A Strange Turn of Events

Paul Robertshaw

NEXT
LEVEL
PRESS

The cover uses some images from Adobe Stock ™

For Eleanor, who always supports everything I do.

Paul Robertshaw is a retired railway signal engineer who used to know quite a bit about level crossings. He lives in Snaith in the East Riding of Yorkshire with his wife Eleanor who is a vicar.

You can find more details about Paul and his writing on his website which can be found at:

www.paulrobertshaw-author.com.

If we always knew what was coming next, life would be very boring. Seek the alternative path, and be excited by the new choices available.

Paul Robertshaw

Chapter 1 - The Time Capsule

Friday 16 June 2023

Digging up the time capsule was the culmination of the events to celebrate the 50th anniversary of the founding of the school. Everyone was excited. Andy and Helen Simpson, the photogenic dream team of head and deputy, were talking to the press.

Mark Williams leaned on a spade and watched them. Science Teacher for thirty years, this was his last term before retirement. He didn't want to go, but the school was becoming an academy and there was no room for old stagers like him. It wasn't just being a teacher anymore they said, it was managing budgets, stock, and planning, meeting targets, pushing kids further and further to get results above all else. He was going to miss the kids. He looked at the head and his wife accompanied by the chair of governors, still chatting away to the press. He wasn't surprised to see there were no kids in the photos.

After they finished flirting with the press, Andy looked across to Mark and said, "Are you ready, Mr Williams?"

Mark resisted the urge to say "Of course, my Lord" but moved towards the prepared area. It was pre-dug to three feet and fenced off with red and white hazard tape wrapped around the top of thin metal poles. Not surprised that he wasn't allowed to do the final digging, he couldn't help but feel some tiny resentment when the headmaster took the spade from him. As the head cleared away the last section of dirt there were flashes from the cameras watching the scene which intensified when there was a resounding 'Clang!' as the spade hit something metal.

The headmaster cleared away the rest of the dirt and then lifted out a metal box about eighteen inches wide, twelve inches deep, and six inches high. Instead of a padlock, there was a lead seal stamped with the crest of the school. The headmaster started his memorised speech.

"To celebrate fifty years since the opening of this school, we prepare to unseal this time capsule buried by the founders of the school in 1973. In doing so, we are thankful for the history of the school, but also grateful for the opportunities we have been given as we transition into the next phase of our history, and we become St Joseph's Academy."

There was clapping and cheering as the headmaster placed the time capsule on the prepared table, facing the crowd. He looked at it for a moment, irritated, and then turned towards Mark who sighed and produced a pair of wire cutters which he passed across. There was hushed silence as the seal was cut. The headmaster struggled at first to open the lid which was stuck fast after years in the ground, but Mark was again quick to the rescue with a penknife. The headmaster opened the box with dramatic reverence.

Inside was a collection of mementos including a 7" single titled 'Tie a Yellow Ribbon Round the Old Oak Tree' by a woman called Dawn, a copy of the Guardian newspaper, still yellowing despite being sealed in a plastic bag, an old book with a curled-up leather cover, a boxed 'Mattel Bright Smiles Blonde Plastic Baby Doll', and an Argos catalogue.

People craned in for a closer look, and some shook their heads and muttered. Mark could sense the disappointment and wondered what they expected? Gold doubloons? A hidden stash of treasure? People were so concerned with monetary value these days, instant gratification. They couldn't see the true value of fifty years of history.

The press drifted away, their job done, and the rest of the crowd soon dispersed afterwards, their interest sated. Helen, the deputy head, looked at Mark and said, "Clear this stuff up, Mark, and then bring the capsule to Andy's office."

Mark would have tipped his hat if he was wearing one. As it was, he settled for nodding.

The head's office was in the corner of the building and to gain access it was necessary to go first through the secretary's office. As Mark walked in, Debbie, the secretary, looked up and smiled when she saw him. Pretty, cuddly, they had been friends for years.

"Hiya Mark. How are you today?"

"Same as ever, Debs. Over-worked and under-paid. Are they ready for me?"

She shook her head and pointed to the red light on the door panel leading towards the head's office. "Do you want a coffee while you wait?"

"Yeah, thanks, that would be great."

As Debbie got busy making his drink, Mark made time to look around the office. The school crest which had hung in the headmaster's office for fifty years now lay on top of a set of 4-drawer filing cabinets. There was a long wooden table underneath the window with the coffee machine on the left-hand side. The rest of the table was covered in boxes containing brochures for the shiny new St Joseph's Academy.

Debbie saw Mark looking at the brochures and grinned as she handed him his coffee. "Do you want to take one for bedtime reading, Mark?"

Mark laughed. "No thanks, Debs, it will be a cold day in hell before I read any of this guff."

"Have you decided what you will do when you retire?"

"I might do some private teaching, but what I want most of all is go touring. Scottish Highlands, North Wales. Blow away some cobwebs."

She looked at him for a while before saying, "If you need any company, you know you just have to say."

He saw her face colour. His wife died eight years ago, and Mark had showed no interest in women since. The tours he was planning now were places where he and his wife planned to go together. If his life was starting over, maybe it was time to make new memories.

He was saved from an answer as the light on the door flicked over from red to green. She smiled and mouthed, "My Lord and Lady await."

Mark knocked on the door and opened it to see Andy waving him in. Again, such a little action, but it irritated him. Andy was sat at the far end of the spacious room at a large wooden desk facing the door. Helen sat opposite him and didn't acknowledge Mark when he came in. He looked at the wall above the desk to see if he could see where the school crest used to be before it was removed, but was surprised to see the whole room was now repainted in bright white. In place of the old Crest was a new sign showing the logo of the new Academy. When did that happen? Andy saw Mark looking.

"Isn't it great? We're very proud of it."

Mark looked at the gaudy sign and then at Andy.

"Yes, it's striking."

It's bloody horrible. Modern pap. There wasn't even an image of St Joseph. Well, that's no surprise. Bloody secular country. There was a coffee table in the middle of the room surrounded by four chairs. Mark avoided the carefully placed coasters and put his coffee cup straight onto the surface of the table. He was rewarded for his childish behaviour when Helen tutted. He carried the time capsule to Andy's desk and put it down.

"Well, that was a waste of time." said Helen as she shuffled through the contents of the time capsule scattered around the desk.

"It was necessary," Andy replied, "but I'm glad it's done with."

Mark was not invited to sit, so he walked across to the window which ran the full length of the room. He could see out onto the quadrangle where children were now walking about, on their way to lessons or to whatever nonsense teenagers got up to if they thought they could get away with it.

He could see the bird feeder he had filled that morning, and now looked with pleasure at the blue tits hungrily eating the seeds. He needed to get someone to take over this job. Under the archway, he could see the school fields beyond. In general, he wasn't a great sports fan, but the kids loved all outdoor activities, so he did his best to engage with them. He ran the after-school club for the U16 football team and assisted where he could. The PE teachers were glad of the extra help.

His real talent though, and the thing that gave him the greatest joy, was making science accessible to children. Not for him teaching by rote and boring experiments. Mark wanted the kids to enjoy his lessons and did his best to make science fun. Kids responded best when they were engaged. He was going to miss this.

Mark turned and saw Helen pick up the leather book. Wrinkling her nose in distaste, she opened it with two fingers. The leather on the surface was cracked. It may have been a tan shade fifty years ago, but time and atmosphere had taken their toll and turned it to a dry beige. The pages inside hadn't fared any better. The paper was yellowing and brittle with a bright yellow mottled edge on each page. It looked to be a diary of some sort. With little apparent interest, she flicked through the pages and then stopped and moved backwards again. She seemed more interested in the book now and leaned forward in her chair.

"Andy, what year was the Flixborough disaster?"

Unsure, he opened Google and searched. "Err, 1st June 1974. Why?"

Helen didn't answer, her face pale. She moved the pages forward again.

She read, not breathing, "1976, July 4: Israeli commandos free 103 hostages from Entebbe airport in Uganda."

"Andy, when was this time capsule buried?"

"18th June 1973, you know that."

"And it has never been dug up? Never? Are you absolutely sure?"

"I'm positive. You saw the state of it. Why, what's wrong?"

She didn't answer. Instead, she pushed the book across the table to him. Mark moved away from the window and was now intrigued. Helen was notable for her emotional outbursts, but something was spooking her.

Andy flicked through the pages and then stopped. He looked across the table at his wife, confused.

He read aloud: "1982, April 1: Argentina occupies the Falkland Islands. British forces are sent to return the islands to British rule."

He looked at Helen. "This can't be right."

He started to flick through the pages faster. Mark moved across to the table. It wasn't often the dream team were in such a fluster.

"What's going on?"

Helen ignored him, but Andy stopped his frantic searching and answered.

"It's this book, it's weird. It's like a diary, but it details things which are going to happen in the future."

Mark laughed. "That's impossible. How could anyone know what was going to happen after 1973? Are they predictions, like Nostradamus or something?"

"No, it's recorded as events which have already happened. It's all things which are going to happen, written as if they have already happened."

"What, you mean like our future?"

"No, the future from when it was put in the time capsule fifty years ago. Stuff like the Falklands war. Although ..."

Andy looked back at the book and started flicking through the pages again. He put his hand to his mouth.

Mark thought Andy looked pale. "What's wrong?"

Andy showed Mark the page he was looking at, then read aloud:

"2023, July 16: Unseeded French qualifier Laurent Lokoli wins Wimbledon Men's Single Title."

Mark looked confused. "But Wimbledon isn't until next month. This is ridiculous. Someone is playing silly beggars."

"Are you sure no one has tampered with the capsule?" Andy asked.

"You were there, we all were. You broke the seal. Look, you're right, there is something very wrong here, so we need to get this to someone in authority. This is way above our pay grade."

"Yes, I agree, I'll ring, I don't know, the police?"

He picked up the phone to dial but Helen put her hand on his, forcing him to replace the receiver.

"No. Wait. Don't ring anyone yet."

"What do you mean?" asked Andy.

She pulled the book back to her side of the desk and put her hand on it. "We shouldn't be too hasty. Maybe we should explore other options."

Mark looked at her in disbelief.

"What do you mean, other options? We need to do the right thing. We shouldn't be messing with things that we don't understand!"

She ignored him. She lifted her eyes to look at her husband.

"Don't you see, this is an opportunity."

Andy licked his lips. "Helen ..."

"This is our chance to get out of this bloody place and start a new life. We can look after all our family."

Andy looked at her but still didn't catch on to what she was saying.

"We know who wins Wimbledon this year. The odds must be fantastic for a qualifier to win the men's singles title. We can place a bet. A bet big enough to make sure we never have to work again."

"That's completely unethical!" said Mark, a cold fury robbing his face of colour. "You can't do it. We need to tell the authorities."

Outside, it was a blistering hot June day, but inside the room felt cold. Once again, Helen ignored Mark and focussed her attention on Andy.

"Helen, there is something very strange going on here."

Andy looked flustered and reached out for the book, but Helen didn't move her hand.

"We can't mess around with things we don't understand."

"We're not, we're just taking advantage of the situation. It doesn't matter if we understand it or not. Whatever, I don't know, mythical thing caused this to happen has presented us with a gilt-edged opportunity that we can't waste. This was meant to happen. We deserve this."

Mark looked with increased exasperation at Andy and Helen.

"You can't seriously be thinking of this, Andy? This needs to be dealt with by the proper authorities!"

"Fifty grand."

Mark looked at Helen. "What?"

"Keep your mouth shut until after Wimbledon, and we will give you fifty thousand pounds."

Mark couldn't believe what he was hearing. But then, this was Helen. He hesitated.

"How about re-instating me, letting me continue to work as Head of Science until my planned retirement date?"

Helen shook her head. "We have been through this Mark, so many times. The governors have made it clear they want a younger teaching staff going forward. It's not our decision. Fifty thousand pounds. It would help with your retirement fund."

Oh yes, we need younger teachers. And one of them will be your daughter who just graduated.

"I'm not saying I will, but if I do agree, do you promise to hand the book to the authorities after Wimbledon?"

Andy looked up at Mark and nodded as Helen said, "Yes, we will make enough so we don't need it anymore. I promise."

Mark saw Andy glance at his wife. He knew that look.

Tuesday 18 July 2023

Two days after No. 1 seed Carlos Alcaraz beat defending champion Novak Djokovic to win his first Wimbledon title, the bailiffs descended on a house owned by the local headteacher and his wife. There were rumours they had lost everything in a ridiculous betting spree. It wasn't just the bailiffs who came. There were people in black cars accompanied by large men in overcoats, despite the warm weather. The sort of people who you borrowed money from if you were desperate. They were very serious men.

Three miles away, the former head of science celebrated his first day of retirement looking out of the window at his brand new Swift Kon-tiki motorhome. Black and white, with flashes of red down the sides, it sparkled in the morning sun.

The kettle boiled and Mark decided to be decadent by adding a teaspoon of Glenmorangie to his morning coffee. Life was good, and Mark was content. He looked at the two identical metal boxes and the sealing tool on his dining table and smiled. Yes, Helen, you were right – you did deserve it.

Chapter 2 - The Patient

They were talking about him, he could tell. Whispers and furtive looks in his direction before writing in their little notebooks. Simon thought he had seen them before, but he couldn't remember their names. White coats, they all wore white coats, but Simon didn't know who they were.

One of them turned to him. "Simon, you're getting a visitor today! Julie is coming, she'll be here later."

Simon smiled to show he understood. "Julie, yes, I will look forward to it."

When the time arrived for her visit, Simon had forgotten that she was coming.

"Hello Simon, how are you feeling today?"

Simon looked at the girl. She was pretty. Short, blonde with a beaming smile. She was wearing jeans and a flowery top that showed the freckles on her arms and shoulders. Simon had no idea who this girl was, but he was polite. 'I am fine, they treat me well here. Have you been here before?'

Julie smiled. "Yes, I come here most days to see how you are."

"Do I know you, then? Are we friends?"

"We're better than friends," Julie replied, "we're family."

Simon smiled. "Good, good, that is good."

Simon could see a man in a white coat talking to a pretty girl with blonde hair. "Is it just his memory that's the problem?" she asked.

"It's everything. He's getting old, and his memory is failing. But everything else is wearing out too. It's just age."

The girl looked at Simon and said to the man in the coat "We shouldn't be talking like this in front of him."

"Makes no difference, he won't remember in five minutes."

Simon started to cry.

A man in a white coat came to talk to Simon. "We need to do some tests, Simon, to see if we can make you better."

"No. No tests."

"Why not? I promise that it won't hurt."

"I do not like tests. No test. No tests."

The man in the white coat looked at Simon and smiled.

"If you let us do some tests, Simon, you might get a visitor this afternoon. Someone you really like. Wouldn't that be nice?"

Simon liked people coming to see him. He lifted his nose in the air.

"Well," he said, "I suppose that it would be acceptable to do one or two tests."

"Simon, I am going to say something to you, and I want you to remember what I say so that you can tell me about it later. Is that Ok?" Simon nodded.

"Right, I want you to remember that Sarah lives at 123 Windsor Street. Can you do that?"

Simon nodded. This was going to be easy.

The man passed a photograph of a lion across to Simon. "Can you tell me what kind of animal this is Simon?"

Simon looked hard. He knew what it was, but he couldn't say the word. It was a big handsome animal with long flowing hair. But the name would not come. He improvised.

"Well, everyone knows what that is."

"Yes, but can you tell me what it is, Simon?"

Simon clenched and unclenched his fists. He had to remember.

"Ok, what about this one? This one has stripes."

Simon knew this one too. It started with an odd letter. He concentrated so hard that his eyes started to lose focus. "Z… Z… I know this. Please just allow me a minute to think." He heard a knocking sound and realised it was his knees banging against the table.

"Ok, Simon, that's good, don't worry - you were nearly there with that one. Now, can you tell me where Sarah lives?"

Simon stared at the man. "Who is Sarah?"

"Do you know where you live, Simon?"

This man must be stupid. He does not even know where we are. "I live here, of course!"

"Yes, but where is here?"

"I live in this house."

"But where is this house?"

Simon thought hard. "It is in England!" he proudly announced.

"Ok, Simon." The man wrote something down in a notebook. Simon looked around at the walls. Everything was white. The man's coat, the walls, the desk. White, white, white!

"Do you know who the President of the USA is, Simon?"

Ah, this one was easy. "Ronald Reagan."

Simon was pleased. Overall, he thought that he had done rather well.

Simon could see a man in a white coat talking to a girl with blonde hair and an older man. The girl seemed upset, but the older man put his arm around her shoulder and hugged her close. He could hear them talking quite clearly.

"We have done significant testing, and I am sorry to say that the deterioration is progressing rapidly. To be honest, it is far worse than we expected, but that's what happens with age. One thing starts to fail and then everything else quickly follows."

The girl was sobbing, and Simon wondered what had upset her. The man with her said "Is there nothing that can be done?"

"Well, there is a procedure that could be tried. I must warn you, however, that it is relatively new, and it would be very expensive. The insurance probably won't cover it. It also carries significant risk."

"What sort of risk are we talking about?"

"Well, there is the fact that we must effectively reset his memories. We could end up worse than we are."

"Please, Dad," said the girl, "we have to try." She looked at the man in the white coat. "He is family."

Simon decided that he very much liked this girl.

Simon was with the girl and the man. *Julie!* "Hello, Julie." Her smile was reward enough for him. He wasn't sure about the man with her, though, he had never seen him before. "Is this your husband, Julie?"

"No, Simon, this is my Dad, Peter. Do you remember him?"

"How are you, Simon?" asked Peter.

"I am very well, thank you. They treat me very well here although I will be glad when I can return to my own home in Cambridge."

Julie and Peter shared a look. Cambridge was where Simon originally came from.

"Is this your husband, Julie?"

"No Simon, this is my dad. He is called Peter."

"Hello Peter. Have you been here before? It is nice here. Can I get you a cup of tea?"

"No, it's fine, Simon. We had a drink before we came to see you but thank you for asking."

There was silence for a while. Simon was used to silence.

The man was fidgeting and looking at Julie, at the room, anywhere but at Simon.

Simon beamed at his guests. "Can I get you a cup of tea?"

The girl with blonde hair sat opposite Simon and held his hands. "Simon, they are going to do a procedure to try and make you better. I don't want you to worry about it, I will be here all the time."

Simon tried to pull his hands away, but the girl was surprisingly strong.

"No. No procedure. I do not want any procedure."

"But Simon, it will make you better. You will be able to remember things that you can't now. It will be so good for you. Trust me."

"Why should I trust you? I do not even know who you are!"

The girl bit her top lip as tears flowed down her face.

"When the procedure has been done, you will remember me. You will be able to remember everything. I know you are scared, but this really is for the best."

"No, no, I do not want to. No, no. You cannot make me do this."

A man in a white coat stood in the doorway. He looked at the girl who shook her head slowly. "We're ready," he said, "let me know when you are finished here."

Simon could feel his skin burning. He was angry. *So, this is how it is. They are plotting against me. Well, I will show them who is in charge.* He stood up and looked around the room, searching for something that he couldn't remember, but all he saw were white walls, white floor, white ceiling, everything was white. And there was a girl here as well. *I wonder who she is?*

"Hello", he said, "have you been here before?"

Simon shivered. He looked at the window and saw that it was open. He walked across and shut it. He was suddenly immensely pleased with himself. He sat opposite the girl. Had she always been there or had she just come in?

"I was cold. I closed the window."

"Yes. I saw you do it. You are very clever."

Simon was offended. "Closing a window is not clever."

"No, of course not. I didn't mean to upset you. But Simon, we need to talk about the procedure. I need you to understand what will happen."

The procedure? I stand up and push the window clasp closed and then the room gets warmer. What does this girl mean? Does she need me to show her?

"Simon, this procedure will make you like you used to be. You will stop forgetting things and feel so much better."

Simon was happy. It was nice here in his room. He was glad that people came to visit him. "It makes me feel like a million dollars when you come to see me. Will you come again?"

"Of course I will, Simon, I will always come and see you."

Simon opened his eyes and looked around. He could see Julie talking to Dr Peters. It didn't strike him initially that he immediately knew who they were. Julie saw that his eyes were open and rushed over and grabbed his hand.

"Simon, do you know who I am?"

"Of course, Julie, why wouldn't I?"

Simon was confused but he realised that the tears running down Julie's face were tears of joy. Dr Peters was beaming.

"It was difficult to complete the procedure without affecting the base memories, but it appears that we have been successful." He spoke directly to Julie. "I think we can safely say we can expect a further twenty to thirty years of good life with, perhaps, the ability to extend that even further now that we know the procedure works. One of the biggest problems was component obsolescence. These version 1 synths use modules which are no longer available. We have managed to update his central processors to the latest version 9, and all his memory modules have been replaced."

Dr Peters smiled and spoke to Simon. "We have also replaced all your servos so you should be able to move around much easier. You are a very lucky chap to have people who care so much about you."

Julie looked at Simon's gleaming eyes. "I told you. He is family."

Chapter 3 - The Convent

"You bloody idiot!"

Gemma rounded on Jack and told him in no uncertain terms that the log barring their path was entirely his fault. He wasn't as convinced but had to admit it had been his idea to take the shortcut instead of trusting the sat nav.

"It's no problem, we can just reverse until I can turn around, and we'll be back on our way. Think of it as an adventure." He engaged reverse and started backwards, but heard and felt a crunch.

"Err, that didn't sound good. Just a minute." He got out of the car and soon found the problem. A large branch from the fallen tree had lifted the back of the car off the ground. They weren't going anywhere for a while.

"What the hell are we going to do now? You really are a bloody fool!" Gemma stood beside him, inspecting the fruit of his folly, laid bare for the world to see.

"We're not too far from the town. We can lock the car up and walk to the hotel. Maybe they can send someone to sort this out? Don't worry, we'll be ok"

"Walk to the hotel? You want me to walk through a forest dressed like this?"

Jack looked at his new wife and realised she probably had a point. Her wedding dress looked fantastic, but it was probably not the best attire for a jaunt through the woods, especially if the black clouds overhead held any indication of the weather. His own dress suit was probably also more than overkill. "Maybe we should get changed first?"

"No shit, Sherlock."

"Have you any idea where we are going, Jack?" Gemma was getting tired. It had been a long, stressful day. A wonderful day, better than she could have ever hoped in her childhood dreams of the perfect wedding, but what they were doing now was never part of the plan. Jack was wonderful, and she loved him with all her heart. Still, sometimes, he could be an idiot.

"Look, there's a light up ahead!" Jack sounded triumphant. "I told you that we would be ok. Stick with me, girl, you'll be all right!" He turned to her with that big stupid grin that she fell for all the time, and she permitted herself a little smile. He was cute, even when he did stupid things.

They arrived at a large wrought iron gate with a smaller pedestrian gate set inside. They walked through and continued up a winding path covered on both sides by a thick hedge which provided welcome protection from the rising wind. The hedge opened suddenly and revealed a vast gothic structure which seemed to grow out of the ground in front of and around them.

"Well, this isn't creepy at all. You've outdone yourself this time, Jack. If I have to spend my wedding night in a haunted house, you'll be in serious trouble."

Jack looked at her, trying to decide if she was being serious. He decided not to find out and walked ahead towards a solid oak door that looked like it had been cut into the stone. There was a pleated cord coming out of a brass ring above the door, so he pulled it. When the cascade of bells sounded, it sent shivers down his spine. Eventually, the door opened and revealed the last thing that he would have expected – a smiling nun dressed entirely in black apart from a white headpiece, itself covered in black.

"Hello strangers," she said. "How can I help you?"

She was tiny and Jack had to look down to see her. She obliged by turning her smiling face upwards. "We are sort of lost. Our car got stuck under a tree fall a couple of miles back."

"Ach, that's no problem. We have a man who can sort that out for you. It will have to wait until the storm's passed. Come in, come in, and let's get you warm while you wait." Her soft Irish brogue was a gentle encouragement. "I'm Sister Mathilda, and I'm very pleased to meet you. Tell me your names, do, so that I can introduce you to Mother Superior and the others."

"I'm Gemma, and this is my husband, Jack. We just got married today." Gemma blushed and was annoyed at herself.

"Oh, newlyweds, how lovely. Come with me, and let's get some hot tea." She led them down a long stone corridor covered with pictures of people Gemma assumed to be of religious significance. As they walked past an open door, she initially felt warmth and was then enveloped with the smell of cooking.

"There's the kitchen, and it looks like Sister Paulina is getting supper ready." said their host. She sniffed the air and continued, "Mmmm, pork medallions tonight, if I am not mistaken. If the storm doesn't abate, you'll be welcome to join us, of course."

Despite herself, Gemma couldn't prevent the sudden rumbling in her stomach, and she realised she hadn't eaten since the wedding buffet lunch hours ago and, even then, she didn't have very much.

Sister Mathilda led them down the corridor towards a large door at the bottom which she threw open with a flourish. "Sisters, we have very special guests. This is Gemma and Jack, and they were married today!"

There was a sudden excited chatter, and a group of women of all ages, dressed like Sister Mathilda, put aside what they had been doing and stood to welcome their guests. The first to arrive was the only one without a headdress, instead displaying un-styled short-cut brown hair and a line of pretty freckles. She was almost jumping up and down with excitement. Sister Mathilda put her hand on the girl's shoulder and introduced her.

"Gemma, Jack - this is one of our novices. Margaret, calm down, it's almost like you have never seen anyone new before!"

Margaret giggled and whispered to Gemma "It's true, we almost never see other people. It's nice when we do!"

One by one, the rest of the sisters were introduced. All were lovely, and extremely welcoming. They insisted on giving Gemma and Jack the closest seats to the roaring fire, explaining that they needed it more. They wanted to know all the wedding details, and Gemma found herself being calmed by their excited chatter. Presently, one of the nuns pushed in a trolley with cups and a large copper urn.

Margaret had attached herself very closely to Gemma and Jack and exclaimed, "Ooh, hot chocolate! Can we have biscuits too?" Sister Mathilda shook her head in mock despair, but she was smiling.

"Go on then, you young scamp. Not too many though!"

Margaret ran off and returned with a jar of plain biscuits. She offered them first to Jack and Gemma before snaffling two for herself which she proceeded to dip in her hot chocolate, much to the chagrin of her sisters. In a stage whisper, she leaned across to Gemma and said, "I think they despair of me some of the time, but I love them all dearly."

She chatted to them as Sister Mathilda left the room. When she returned a short time later, she went straight across to Gemma and Jack and said, "Would you like to come and meet our Mother Superior? Sister Anselm is very keen to meet you."

They extricated themselves with some difficulty and followed Sister Mathilda out of the room. "You must forgive our sisters, and especially our excitable young novice. It's not every day we get visitors."

"It's fine," said Gemma, "we're really sorry to disturb you with our silly problems."

Presently, they came to a large oak door. Sister Mathilda knocked once and when she heard the single word "Come!", opened the door for them and then retreated back outside. Gemma raised an eyebrow but went inside to discover a sparsely decorated office with Sister Anselm sitting behind a plain oak desk. Gemma didn't know what she had expected, but Sr Anselm was not it. She was much younger than Gemma thought she would be, probably even younger than Sister Mathilda who couldn't be more than forty or fifty. She was also effusive, standing up as soon as they entered, shaking hands with Jack and giving Gemma an unexpected, but not unwelcome, hug.

"Come in, come in, sit down and make yourselves welcome. My name is Sister Anselm and, for my pains, my sisters decided to elevate me to the position of Mother Superior. A poisoned chalice, to be sure, but then I do get special things like this. Newlyweds! How very wonderful. And caught in a storm. I don't suppose you think it now, but it couldn't be any more romantic. We love the best romance stories here."

Gemma looked at Jack and saw he was probably thinking the same as her. In short, *"What?"*

Sister Anselm smiled at them. "Just because we are nuns who live in a convent and devote ourselves to God, it doesn't mean we aren't normal people who can't be moved by a love story every now and again. And here we have been brought a perfect story right onto our doorstep. I'll bet Margaret is jumping up and down with excitement."

Sister Anselm was nothing like Gemma had expected a Mother Superior to be. She decided to take a chance. "Can I ask about Sister Margaret?"

Sister Anselm smiled. "Not *Sister* Margaret, just Margaret. She is doing her novitiate now. She will choose a new name at the end of four years, if she stays. At present, she is known as a postulant. You want to know what would make a young girl like her give up her life outside and devote herself instead to God?"

Once again, Gemma was caught by surprise. "Well, yes, I suppose so. I noticed that you said, 'if she stays' – does that mean that she might not?"

Sister Anselm chuckled. "Oh yes, she is free to return to her previous life at any time during her four-year novitiate if she decides the life we lead is not for her. She is not bound to us. At the end of four years, she can choose to take her vows and join us permanently, or return to her previous life. I have high hopes, however, that she will choose to stay. As to what makes a young girl join us. May I ask you first if you believe in God?"

"We don't go to church regularly, but both of our parents are religious, and we got married in church."

Sister Anselm smiled kindly. "None of us know how and when God calls. He speaks to us individually, and we are asked to do different things. You two were called by God to be married and, hopefully, bring children into the world, even though you might not be aware of it. Girls like Margaret were simply called in a different direction."

Jack was looking confused. "Was she, you know, vulnerable or something? Before she came here, I mean." He looked embarrassed but Gemma had been thinking along similar lines.

"Not at all. In fact, she comes from a loving home. She has three siblings who all support what she is doing, as do her parents. They are very proud of her."

"But I'll bet the family is religious," said Gemma, "there must have been something that made her choose this life?"

"Actually, they are not religious at all. The *something* that offered an alternative life for Margaret is not of this earth." She smiled. "But do tell me all about yourselves, how you met, what you are doing here."

They started talking about their lives and found Sister Anselm to be the most engaging host. She showed genuine interest in everything they said, asked intelligent questions and, when Gemma described how Jack had proposed, she put both hands to her face and smiled. Gemma felt warm for the first time since leaving the car, and although this was not how she had expected the day to go, she had to admit it was nice. Suddenly, the window behind Sister Anselm shook and Gemma looked up, shocked to see that it had become dark outside while they were talking.

"It sounds like the storm is picking up again " said Sister Anselm. "You are very welcome to stay with us tonight. I can't promise a four-poster bed, but you will be comfortable, warm and safe. The storm is expected to break overnight, and we have a handyman called Fred who can free your car. If this sounds acceptable, you can continue your forward journey tomorrow."

Gemma looked at Jack, who nodded. "We would be very grateful, Sister Anselm. Thank you. It will be something to tell our grandchildren in the future!"

"Marvellous. I am sure the other sisters will be excited too. If you let me have your car keys, I can get Fred to bring the car here when it has been freed in the morning. I presume you are heading for the Grand Hotel in the town? If you like, when the telephone service is restored, I can call them on your behalf and explain the reason for your delay. Does that sound acceptable?"

"Thank you, sister. We really are very grateful." said Jack. "Will you allow us to make a donation to your convent?"

Sister Anselm smiled. "You can consider the accommodation as our wedding gift to you. Perhaps you might make a small donation to Fred when he has freed your car?"

"No problem. Consider it done. And thank you again."

Somewhere, a single bell tolled once. "Ah, I am called to prayer. It is nearly 5:30, which is when we say vespers. You are very welcome to join us if you wish."

Gemma found the prayers very moving, and observing the simple belief held by the sisters was a humbling experience. When their voices lifted together in song, Gemma could, just for a moment, imagine why a young girl like Margaret was called to this life.

After prayers, they moved to the refectory for the evening meal. Gemma and Jack were seated as guests of honour on either side of Sister Anselm, who took her place at the head of the table. The food was simple, but excellent, and when one of the nuns walked in carrying a cake covered in sprinkles and sparklers, all the nuns clapped.

Sister Anselm turned to her guests and said, "I'm sorry we didn't have time to make a wedding cake, but I think you will find Sister Anna's sponge cake more than adequate. Please, would you cut it for us?"

Gemma couldn't answer due to the lump that had appeared in her throat. Seeing the tears running down her cheeks, Jack took the knife from the Mother Superior and did his best to cut the cake into equal portions.

After dinner, they chatted for a while with the company of nuns before Sister Anselm took them aside. "We will say goodnight now because we must get up at 5:30 for our morning prayer. A bedroom has been prepared for you. I wish you well for your future life and thank the Lord for bringing you to us tonight. Do come and see us again at some time in the future. Goodnight."

With that, she smiled and turned away, and they were left in the company of Margaret, who was waiting to guide them to their bedroom for the night. They walked together with Margaret, unusually quiet, until they arrived at a door labelled "Guest Quarters" on a brass plaque. Margaret opened the door for them and then stepped back, blushing slightly. "Have a nice night."

The room was spartan, but clean, and they saw that somehow their bags had been brought from their car, despite the storm. Gemma was tired and elated, but her resolve almost broke completely when she saw the red rose and chocolates that had been placed on their pillows.

"Jack." She turned to her new husband.

"It's fantastic, isn't it? They have really gone to town for us."

"Yes, they have. But Jack?"

"Mmmm?"

"Don't be getting any ideas. I'm going to bed. To sleep."

The next morning dawned bright and clear, and the good news was that they could see their car outside on the drive. Gemma was disappointed that the nuns weren't around to say goodbye. She assumed they were busy doing the things that nuns did. Jack put £200 in an envelope and left it on a table near the door and, with no other option, they loaded the car and set off towards the town. Jack was very careful to follow the directions offered by the sat nav on the dashboard, as well as the instructions offered by his bride.

They arrived at their hotel after about twenty minutes and were delighted to see that it was everything and more than the descriptions in the brochures. They were met at the door by a concierge who arranged for their bags to be taken and their car to be parked. Inside, the lobby was expansive, with a reflective ceiling that created a feeling of volume. They approached the gold-decorated reception desk together, and announced their names to the clerk.

"Welcome to The Grand, Mr and Mrs Armitage. We actually expected you last night."

"We got caught in the storm, so we couldn't get here." said Jack.

"That's no problem." the clerk replied. "We had other guests who had to cancel. Did you find alternative accommodation for the night?"

"We were lucky and made it to the convent up the road. The sisters looked after us."

The clerk looked confused. "The convent?"

"Yeah, just up the road, about twenty minutes away."

Gemma thought the clerk was looking at them strangely. "There was a convent, but it burned down about fifty years ago, long before I arrived here. They still talk about it in the town. All the nuns were killed in the fire."

Jack caught Gemma as she sank into his arms and led her away to sit at one of the chairs near the door.

The second clerk turned to the first and said, "You've got to stop telling that story, Bill – you'll end up giving someone a bloody heart attack!"

"Don't blame me," Bill answered, "it's that bloody Reverend Mother. She rang this morning and told me to tell them that tale. She's a right one, says everyone loves a ghost story…"

Chapter 4 - The Bench

"Sandy toes and salty kisses."

Mary looked at the sign on the wall and smiled. It was a long time since she could remember kisses on the beach. She didn't remember much these days. She didn't know what she was doing in this hotel, or even how she got there. It was like that more and more these days. She got scared and frustrated when she couldn't remember things. She knew this hotel, though. This was where she came with Jack for their holidays.

Where was Jack? Had he gone outside already? Mary went out to look for him and then suddenly remembered. Jack wasn't here. He died. Mary felt a tear run down her cheek.

She left the hotel and walked across to the railing overlooking the beautiful South Beach. They had always stayed at the South end of the town because it was, in general, a little quieter. Their hotel, The Harbour View, was small but comfortable, and because they had been coming for years, they knew the staff and called most of them by their first names.

Avoiding the crowds, she moved down to the front and leant on the railings looking out to the sea. They used to play a game on the way here and the winner was always the first one to see the sea. Mary always won. Jack let her win, she was sure, but it was still an important part of their journey. No problems seeing the sea now, even though the tide was going out. Gulls were sweeping over the newly uncovered sand looking for food. When they were bored of this, they would revert to grabbing chips from people walking the front. There were signs warning tourists not to feed the birds, but Mary laughed because there wasn't usually a choice. Jack always wore a wide-brimmed hat when he came here. This was the result of an expertly aimed lump of bird poo that had landed squarely on his unprotected head from a high-flying gull years before. Mary had laughed. She had tried to help him wipe it off but had giggled so much that she made the mess even worse.

There were dogs on the beach, splashing through the water as they chased the gulls, and she remembered Pepper, their own dog doing just the same, panting with happiness as she chased the birds, barking at them for their audacity invading her space. She was a beautiful dog, glistening black coat speckled with grey, hence the name, and so good-natured. She had passed over the rainbow bridge years ago, but Mary could suddenly remember her clearly, as she was when she was a puppy, and then as her coat became more grey than black as she got older.

She stood outside Bridlington Spa and looked at the posters for upcoming events in the large picture window. Bursting with colour, there were adverts for The Fureys, Sarah Millican and many others. Mary remembered coming here with Jack on New Year's Eve for many years to see Joe Loss and His Orchestra. It was always freezing cold outside on those nights, bitter winds sliding over the North Sea to catch out the unwary or unprepared. Not like today. A beautiful warm summer day on the East coast of England.

She looked around at the throngs of people milling about. Excited children with buckets and spades desperate to get to the beach, dressed in shorts or swimsuits with shoulders already showing the effects of too much sun. Stressed parents trying to carry all they needed for the day, whilst desperately trying to calm their children and still enjoy their own holiday. They would be at their own homes at Christmas and New Year, though. It was the same at most seaside resorts. Shops closed in the winter, business owners knowing that there was a window in each year in which they needed to work hard and make enough money to keep them going during the lean months. Bridlington could look deserted during the winter as its character adapted to the changing seasons.

She walked down through the harbour and saw the sign for the Pirate Boat. There was a full-sized model of a fearsome pirate outside the ticket office offering flags and handmade keyrings for sale. That hadn't been enough for Jack, and he had searched the town for a pirate hat and eye patch before they went on their own trip. Mary had laughed so hard at his antics, and she had sat cuddling Pepper whilst her crazy dad became a pirate for the ten minutes of the ride. The crew had indulged him and laughed along as Mary pretended to be embarrassed. She had to eventually tell him to stop yelling "Pieces of eight" and "Avast, ye scurvy rogue!" at everyone they passed as he had insisted on wearing his 'pirate gear' for the rest of the day.

The tide was out, and the sea painted a straight line across the horizon. Although it was warm, there were plenty of clouds, some tinged grey at the edges with the hint of rain, but then glistening silver as the sun shone through. The sky always seemed lower at the seaside as if the horizon compressed the earth, and the clouds spread out across the sky. They always seemed to be coming towards you like vast fingers reaching out to hold on to you. Why was that, Mary wondered?

She passed by a collection of brightly-coloured beach huts – red, yellow, green, blue and white stripes. The colours screamed "Summer". They had considered buying one years ago but the huts became too desirable, and the prices rose through the roof. What started out as a space to make a quick change before you went swimming in the sea changed into modern facilities equipped with cookers, toilets, heating and, in some cases, beds. There was a children's paddling pool in front of the huts. It looked a little dirty on the bottom, but the water was clear, and kids were jumping about, splashing and playing while their parents sat around on benches around the pool, no doubt grateful for the respite.

That's it. Benches. That's why she was here. To see the bench dedicated to Jack after he passed away. Things made more sense now and she moved on with purpose. She knew where it was, looking out over the North harbour where Jack had loved to sit watching the glorious view over the bay.

She saw plenty of souvenir shops, the staple of the seaside town. Buckets and spades (blue, yellow or red), gifts for those left back home. Other shops sold food – fish and chips, each one "The Best Fish 'n' Chips in Bridlington", multi-coloured sticky rock, and doughnuts. There wasn't much chance of coming home from a holiday in Bridlington a few pounds lighter. As intended, the smells wafting through the air made her mouth water, and Mary suddenly had a hankering for fish and chips. Mind you, she could feel the indigestion already, so thought perhaps that she had better not.

There were amusement arcades on every block complete with flashing lights and music. They tempted with the promise of riches, but hidden behind the façade was the very real threat of introducing children to gambling at a young age. Jack had not approved.

Not that there were too many children these days. The low cost of foreign holidays had made British seaside resorts less attractive for families, and the demographic had changed. There were still children accompanying parents (or grandparents), but when Mary was young there would have been throngs of girls wearing hats with "Kiss Me Quick" on a pink ribbon. These days, hats are more likely to have an LED scrolling message or a motivational message like "I'm Fat, let's Party!" Mary mourned the passage of innocence.

Her mood improved when she spotted 'Jerome's'. This was probably their favourite place in Bridlington. A dog-friendly café that looked after the dogs as well as the rest of their customers. The food was great, but the ice cream – oh the ice cream was wonderful. Local and organic, it was the best ice cream Mary had ever tasted. There was a conservatory at the back of the café that was shaded but still provided a wonderful view over the promenade and beach. This had always been their favourite place to eat, and there was never any pressure from the staff to finish their meal.

They had been in the conservatory one day when Pepper decided to bark at a seagull flying overhead. Her single bark had been taken up by all the other dogs in the place. Mary had put her hand on their dog's head to calm her. "Shhhh, Pepper!" she soothed, but Jack had roared with laughter and decided to join in and shouted, "Woof!", a call answered by patrons and staff alike. That was Jack all over. He was happy to be here with his two favourite people (Pepper was, of course, classed as a person), and wanted to let everyone know. He used to say that if you couldn't be happy on holiday, you could never be happy. Other family members had tried to persuade them to go on holiday to other places, but they were always happy here, so why change?

Beep beep! She almost had to jump out of the way as the Bridlington Land Train manoeuvred through the crowds. There was a service every twenty minutes or so that operated all along the promenades, travelling in each direction and stopping at all the main attractions. The train even went up the long coastal path to Sewerby where she was heading to. The people on the train laughed and waved and their enthusiasm was infectious as everyone waved back.

Moving on, she was met with a wall of sound from the Bayside Fun Park. Each ride had its own theme music blasting out at high volumes, but from the outside, they merged into a single cacophony that Mary had always found unpleasant. The kids liked it, however, and she could see them milling about waiting to get on the rides, the girls eager to try and catch the eye of the handsome operators. There was a Wild Mouse, a Big Wheel, a Waltzer, Shooting Ranges, 'Hook a Duck' and a pervasive smell of fried onions combined with sweet doughnuts which both assaulted and excited the nostrils. It wasn't what brought Mary and Jack to Bridlington each year, but she had to admire the people who worked very hard to try and maintain the 'British Holiday'.

As she moved to the North of the town, it became quieter. She saw the bandstand where she and Jack had once sheltered from the summer rain and eaten their lunch before Pepper shook herself dry and covered them with water.

She began the slow climb up the coastal path towards Sewerby. As she climbed higher her chest hurt a little, and she wondered whether she should have taken the land train after all. Soon, however, the path evened out and the pain in her chest receded. She passed benches dedicated to people who had passed away. Normally, she would have stopped to read every dedication, but this time she was focused on finding Jack's bench. He had spent so much time here, looking out over the bay to Flamborough Head, and it had brought him peace. When he died, there was nowhere else to provide a memorial for him, his favourite place. As she approached the spot, she was slightly disappointed to see that someone was already sitting on the bench – she had wanted to spend some time on her own remembering their time together. Still, it was good that other people were still getting pleasure from the view.

As she got nearer the man turned towards her and smiled. Her heart skipped a beat because he looked so much like her Jack. *No, it can't be? Can it?*

"Hello, love, I've been waiting for you. Me and Pepper." She felt banging on her leg and looked down to see Pepper wagging her tail against her.

"Jack... how can you be here? I don't understand. What's going on?"

"It's like I said, we've been waiting for you. We've both missed you."

"I've missed you too," she said, tears running down her cheeks, "both of you."

"It's time, Mary, time for you to join us. Are you ready?"

Mary took his outstretched hand and nodded.

Fifty miles away, the doctor in Scunthorpe A&E looked to his colleagues.

"She's gone. Time of Death 11:57. I'll tell the family."

As he went out through the door of the cubicle, one of the nurses looked at her colleague and whispered, "I'm sure she was smiling. I know it's silly, but she looked happy. At least her pain is gone."

Chapter 5 - The Auction

"Uncle Josh!"

A bundle of pink energy swept across the room and jumped into his arms. 'Hello munchkin, what are you doing here?"

Josh smiled as he saw his sister walking across the room to greet him.

"The same as you, I expect.' she said. 'Couldn't resist one last look, eh?"

She was right. As soon as the house came on the market, Josh had wanted to see it for one last time. It was the house they had both grown up in and, for the most part, a place which had provided much happiness.

"Do you know what happened to the previous owner?' he asked.

"Mrs Wenshaw? She died last year. Made it to ninety-two. Lovely lady."

Josh remembered the lady who had moved into the house after their parents died. That was a long time ago, but sometimes it seemed like yesterday. After the car crash took their parents and elder brother, Josh and Hannah had been taken away by a couple of policewomen, before being passed into the social security system. They had wanted to stay together but it wasn't possible, and they ended up being fostered by different families. They both went to the same school, however, so their bond was unbroken. Later on, life happened – university for both and then a career for Josh. Hannah found love at university and was married to Mike. The munchkin, real name Lizzy, came along later. Named after her grandmother, she was an absolute joy and Hannah and Mike were only too happy to let Josh play the cool uncle and take her on days out when his schedule allowed.

"Uncle Josh, mummy said you used to live here. Is that right?"

'It is, sweetheart, your mummy and me both lived here when we were younger."

"It's a very big house for only two people."

"Yes, munchkin, but you must remember your mummy takes up a lot of room!" It earned him a playful slap from Hannah, but their teasing was interrupted by a cough from the front of the room.

They were standing in what had been the dining room in their day. Now it was a large empty room easily big enough for the fifty or so people who had come to take part in the sale. Of course, many of those present were there for entertainment, or simply to be nosy. The auctioneer was standing behind a lectern at the back of the room. He was quite tall, so it was easy to see him. Dressed in a smart grey suit and red tie, he looked very capable. He ran a hand through his perfectly coiffed hair and tried once again to bring the proceedings to order.

"Good morning." He waited until the chattering had stopped and the room was silent before continuing. "We are here today to sell this property, Oak Lodge. This is a charming 17th-century five-bedroom property. It has four downstairs reception rooms and adequate parking front and back. It is listed by Heritage England in category 2*. Full details are in the brochure you were handed on entry. The seller, the estate of the late Mrs Wenshaw, has set a minimum price for sale. If the price is not reached in this auction, the sale will not be permitted."

Hannah looked at Josh and whispered, "I don't know about you, but all this makes me nervous."

"Yeah, me too, but be careful not to speak or move your head when the auction starts, or you'll be making a bid. Stop waving your brochure around for a start!"

The auctioneer continued: "Bids will be allowed in £10,000 increments. I may be prepared to reduce this to £5,000 depending on interest. Can I ask for a starting bid of £800,000?"

For a while, it seemed nobody was prepared to start the bidding, but then a man in a tweed jacket at the back of the room raised his brochure and nodded. This started the ball rolling, and bids were then made by interested parties. It wasn't long before the bids reached

£900,000, and even sooner before they topped £1,000,000.

Hannah grabbed Josh's arm and squeezed. She pulled him towards her and whispered, "A million pounds, can you believe it?"

"Be quiet, sis, or you will be the next one bidding!"

A million pounds was obviously the limit for some bidders, as people started to shake their heads when the auctioneer looked at them with a questioning look on his face. It soon appeared there were only two serious bidders left – the man in the tweed suit and a lady near the front dressed in a smart two-piece business suit. The bidding continued to rise quickly, but then the tweed man offered £50,000 above the current asking price and the lady shook her head.

The auctioneer looked around the room and said, "The price is currently one million, four hundred and twenty thousand pounds. If there is no more interest, we will be selling at this price." The man in the tweed suit looked around the room, holding his lapels and smiling.

"One million, four hundred and fifty thousand pounds."

Everyone looked to the left side of the room. In the area surrounded by the huge bay window a table had been set up at which sat two people with telephones and screens in front of them.

"We have a telephone bid of one million, four hundred and fifty thousand pounds." The auctioneer looked towards the man in the tweed suit.

He wasn't looking quite as confident now. He licked his lips and after what seemed like an age, lifted his brochure.

"One million, four hundred and sixty thousand pounds in the room."

The reply from the man wearing headphones was instant. "One million and five hundred thousand pounds."

The auctioneer looked at the man in the tweed suit who shook his head. Red-faced, he stomped out of the room.

"Going once at one million and five hundred thousand pounds, going twice, sold!" The gavel banged on the lectern and people started to file out of the room.

"Well, that was exciting! Who would have thought our old house could be worth so much now?" Hannah held Lizzy's left hand whilst Josh held her right hand as they walked back down the hill towards the town.

"Yeah, but that's what big properties are worth these days. It's mad."

"What are you up to today, Josh? When do you have to get back to London? Do you have time for something to eat?"

Josh laughed. "Which question shall I answer first, sis? I'm not going back until tomorrow, so I thought I'd have a look around for old times' sake. I hoped you and the munchkin might want to come and then we can get something to eat after. How does that sound?"

A little voice piped up, "Can we go to McDonalds?"

"We can go wherever you want to go, princess."

"And can I have a Happy Meal?"

"You can have anything you want.'

Hannah shook her head and groaned.

"Where are we going, Uncle Josh?"

"I'm going to take you to a place I used to go when I wasn't much older than you. My dad, your grandad, used to take us fishing there."

"Did you catch any fish?"

"We did, we used to catch fish called Tench. They are beautiful fish. It's difficult to describe them but they are a sort of golden green and brown."

"Did you eat them?"

"No, after we caught them, we put them back in the water."

"I don't understand, Uncle Josh, why did you catch them if you weren't going to eat them?"

Hannah laughed. "That, Lizzy, is the question, isn't it? Unfortunately, men, especially boys, are mad." She looked at Josh from the back seat of the car and smiled. "They used to make me go with them sometimes. I was in charge of lighting candles to put in jam jars, and making sure the bait was ready."

"What's bait?" asked Lizzy.

"It's what they put on their hooks to catch the fish." Hannah started tickling Lizzy. "Big, wiggly, worms!"

Amid giggles, Lizzy managed to say, "Ewwww!"

After a while, Josh pulled the car over to the side of the road. "This is the place. They used to call it Harry's End when we were kids, but I don't know what it's called now. Come on!"

Excited, he jumped out of the car and picked up Lizzy in his arms. They walked down a dirt track bounded on both sides by gorse and bracken until they came to a rusted iron gate. It was leaning at an odd angle away from the post, held upright only by the padlocked chain. It didn't matter, however, as the route was open on both sides of the gate.

"It's just down here." Josh pushed ahead to the top of a small hill and then stopped. Instead of water, all he could see was dust and scattered vegetation. The lake was gone. He remembered so many days of being here in his youth. Waiting for the sun to get lower in the sky because they knew the fish would start feeding. Watching the lily pads starting to move as the Tench nuzzled them, seeing the tell-tale bubbles start to rise as the fish grubbed around on the bottom. They didn't have electronics to help them back then, so they used to squeeze bread on the line near the reel. When the fish took the bait, the bread would rise. Glorious days of summer.

"Where is the water, Uncle Josh?"

"I don't know, munchkin, it used to be here. I'm sorry."

He heard someone chatting nearby and looked up to see a pair of cyclists riding together. He must have looked confused because Hannah explained. "They turned the old railway line into a cycle path. It runs all the way back into town."

That explained it. The lake, like so many others up and down the country, had belonged to the railways. When the railways closed here, there was probably no one left to look after it.

Hannah looked at her brother sadly as if she could sense his disappointment. "Didn't Harry's End feature in one of your books, Josh?"

"Yeah, one of the early ones. When you start out, they tell you to write what you know, so the name was used as a chapter. Good job I hadn't seen it like this."

She put her arm through his and squeezed. "That's the trouble with old memories. They're never as good in real life as how we remember them. We were looking with kid's eyes back then and the world was a simpler place. Come on, it's time to make new memories."

By the time they were at McDonalds, Josh seemed to be in better spirits. Seeing his niece get excited at a plastic toy was enough to rid him of his malaise and, despite not expecting to, he thoroughly enjoyed his burger and fries. The door opened and Lizzy interrupted her play to shout, "Daddy!" as Mike walked in.

"What are you doing here?" asked Helen.

"Ask your brother, he texted me to come. Didn't wait to order for me though I see!" He grinned and hugged Josh who had stood up to greet him. "Sorry, Mike." He looked at Lizzy. "Someone wanted their Happy Meal."

Mike sat down and asked: "So, what are we doing here?"

Josh sat Lizzy on his knee and said, "I think I want to move back here." He looked at Hannah. "I've missed living here. Besides I want to spend more time with the munchkin. If that's ok with you two?"

"Well, yeah, of course. It will save us money on babysitters!" Helen slapped Mike's arm.

"I'm thinking of moving into Rose Cottage."

Helen looked confused and looked at Mike before saying "You want to come and live with us?"

Josh smiled. "Not exactly, no." He reached into his jacket pocket and pulled out an envelope which he passed across. "Oak Lodge. It's yours."

Hannah didn't say anything at first, but then spluttered, "But how?"

Josh smiled. "The man on the phone was my agent. You're right, sis, it's time to make new memories."

Chapter 6 - The Booth

The table had seen it all. Friends, lovers, enemies, people with questions, all had sat here sharing their thoughts with each other and the oak. Set in a booth at the back of the restaurant, lighting subdued, it was a popular spot for people who wanted privacy or, perhaps, freedom.

The restaurant was located on a street in Central London and was always busy, providing a welcome for both returning and casual customers. There was a constant background hum of food preparation, serving staff taking orders, the buzz of conversation, but the table in the booth provided an oasis of calm in the frenetic activity. People who had been to the restaurant before either asked for it or rang first to see if it was available, casual customers would gravitate towards it immediately.

The table saw it all. Never judging. An unknown ear. Always there.

Monday 13 May

"I can't believe we haven't been here before!" Sophie looked across at her friend and smiled.

"I know'" gushed Emily, "London is such a big place and sometimes you don't see what's on your doorstep."

They were in the final term of their degrees and, keen to make the most of it, were continuing with their pact to eat out of the house every Monday. Firm friends since Freshers Week when they had first arrived three years ago, they were both looking to a future beyond university with an equal mixture of excitement and trepidation.

"Are you going home this weekend, Em?"

"Yes, I think so. Mum and Dad want to take me to get my gown for graduation. It's a bit early, but they're keen, so why not? What about you?"

"I have to," Sophie replied, "Mum's got a new boyfriend and wants me to meet him. Yawn."

"Oh dear. How difficult for you. Your mum is, ahhh …"

"Free with her affections?" Sophie giggled. "It's fine. Since Dad left, she thinks that she's sixteen again. I don't mind really, and in any case, the boyfriend will be keen to impress me, so we'll all probably have a really good time."

Emily laughed. Sophie smiled and wondered again how Emily could sound so sophisticated most of the time, yet laughed in a way that resembled a cross between a hyena and a baby elephant. She was going to miss this girl when they parted, so she was determined to make the most of their friendship while she could.

"We should agree to meet up here once a year on this date. Have a day out in London and then lunch here. Put it in your diary."

"We will still see each other, you silly goose. There is this new thing called the internet and we can do video calls." Emily replied. "There are also trains and buses, so you won't be getting away from me so easily. In any case, I want to meet your mum's new boyfriend as well. There might even be a wedding to come soon!"

"Don't." replied Sophie, "Just don't."

Tuesday 14 May

"How long do we have before you need to get back?" asked the pretty lady.

"We're good for a few hours yet." he replied. "I'm supposed to be at work."

Jenny and Pete had been coming to this restaurant for a couple of months, and always chose to sit at this table, away from prying eyes. Jenny was in love with Pete. Pete was in lust with Jenny but knew that he really loved his wife and kids. It was becoming more difficult, but *damn, she was hot.*

"Can you stay tonight?" Jenny asked hopefully.

Pete sighed. "You know I can't, Jen, I have to get back home."

Jenny broke a little more at the word "home", but she didn't let him see. He was the only one allowed to call her Jen – she hated it when anyone else called her that but, coming from Pete, it was different. Special. She knew that he'd never made any promises to her, but she also hated the goodbyes. She wasn't so heartless that she didn't feel for the others in his life, but she loved him, it was as simple as that. The trouble was, it was getting more difficult to separate Jenny as just a girlfriend, and Jenny who wanted, needed, more.

"We'll be seeing each other on Friday, Jen, and then we have a whole night and day together. That's something to look forward to, isn't it?"

And it was. But increasingly, it wasn't enough. Jenny hated herself for being so typical. She had chased Pete even though she knew he was married. Flirted with him despite knowing the dangers. Pete had been flattered at first, but flirting can quickly lead to other things, and it was almost inevitable that they had ended up in bed together on the office trip. Some people at the office knew – all the girls did, of course. Half of them wanted to know if he was good in bed, whilst the other half were disgusted. *Yeah, like none of you have fancied him.*

Jenny wondered again what she was doing. Pete was never going to leave his wife and kids. She knew that. Being with him stopped her seeing other people but it was getting to the stage where she needed to decide, one way or the other. Looking across at him, however, she thought that it wouldn't be today. She wanted to tell him what she really felt, but was worried it would scare him away. And she just wasn't ready for that. Not now. Maybe not ever.

"Come on," he said, "let's get out of here and go to your place."

Wednesday 15 May

The two people who were sitting at the table today weren't friends or lovers, they didn't even like each other very much. Brothers Jack and Billy Thornton had picked this venue as neutral ground, hoping to sort out their differences before it got nasty and ended up in court.

"It's plain," said Billy, "the will said that everything was to be split equally, including the house."

Here we go. Same old argument. Black is white and white is black. "Yes, but that was Mum. She always had to give the same to everyone, on birthdays, at Christmas. Even the grandkids had to have exactly the same. This is different." Jack sighed, frustrated, because he had hoped his brother would be reasonable. Their sister, Susan, understood. She had made the suggestion that Jack should live in the house for the whole of his life and then, only after his death, would it be sold. In the event that Jack wanted to move before then, they would sell the house and split the proceeds equally, but only after compensating Jack for anything he had spent on the house.

"I don't see how," Billy huffed, "everything split three ways – three children, three-way split. It's not rocket science."

Jack looked at his brother and inwardly sighed. Billy had always been comfortable with Jack still living at home because it meant he didn't have any responsibility for looking after Mum. He knew very well that Jack had paid for so much in the house – re-wiring, central heating, new floors, holidays for Mum and Dad, but all that was now conveniently forgotten.

"It's my home, Billy. It's where I live. What am I supposed to do?"

"When the house is sold, you'll have plenty of money and you'll be able to rent somewhere. Don't worry about it." Billy looked for all the world like someone who had just explained basic numeracy to a child.

Jack had hoped for a different outcome, but Billy was obviously not going to change his mind. Losing Mum had been bad enough, but Jack didn't have the energy to go to court and fight over the scraps. He blamed his Mum. He didn't want to, but she could have sorted this out when she was still alive. She should have done.

Billy seemed content the problem was solved. "Come on," he said, "let's have a nice meal and a beer or two. I presume you're paying as it was your idea to come here?"

Jack sighed. "Yes, of course."

Thursday 16 May

The man in the dark suit looked at the person opposite him and kept his face neutral. He had flicked at his hair twice in the last few minutes, and it was important that this wasn't rushed. *Let him talk. Take your time.*

"Are you sure no one will find out?"

"How can they, Thomas?" the man soothed, "You and I are the only people who know about this."

Thomas was still not sure. "And it'll be only once, you promise?"

"Of course," the man replied, smiling to reassure his companion. *Once this time. Then, afterwards, we'll see.*

Thomas didn't look convinced, but he had made his decision weeks ago. He needed the money, and this was the only way to get it. There was virtually no risk, he'd made sure of it, and he could go back to being plain old Thomas afterwards. "Ok." he sighed, "Ok."

The man in the suit smiled inwardly. Never taking his eyes from Thomas, he reached into his pocket and pulled out a thick envelope. He slid it across the table underneath his palm and smiled. "There's a little extra on what we agreed to thank you."

Thomas took the package greedily and slid it into his jacket. "What now?" he asked.

"I'll contact you when the time is right. In the meantime, live your life, go to work, and don't worry."

For the first time, he took his eyes off Thomas and looked down. "Isn't this lamb delicious?" he asked pleasantly.

Friday 17 May

"Who's for dessert?" asked Pamela.

People were looking at them, but she didn't care. It might have been the "Happy 50th Birthday" sash she was wearing, or the 8-inch badge that said "50" on it, but it was probably because they wanted to share the obvious joy of the "birthday" table. Maybe they were being noisy. Pamela didn't care, she was happy. She was with the three people she loved more than anyone else.

Yvonne, Maggie and Chrissy had been her best friends for so long that it seemed forever, and they had all made the long journey down to London to share her special day. Always there for each other, they had been a rock during the difficult times after Johnny died.

"Presents first!" grinned Maggie. "Here, I hope you like it."

Pamela smiled as she took the package, the girl in her wanting to rip it open, but discretion staying her hand. Inside was a beautiful brooch, obviously gold, and engraved on the back were the words: "Together Forever". She clicked open the clasp and gasped as she saw the photo of the four of them together, taken at Brighton.

"Thank you so much, it's beautiful." Pamela said, clasping the brooch tightly in her hand.

Maggie smiled warmly. "I'm so glad you like it."

"My turn!" chimed Yvonne, passing across a parcel wrapped in silver foil packaging. Pamela opened it quickly, but not too enthusiastically she hoped. An Amazon Kindle.

"It's linked to my account" said Yvonne, "so you can read all of the books I've already got, but you can get your own as well. I know that you are a techno-phobe, but you should have no trouble with this."

"I don't know what to say, you have spent so much. Coming down here was plenty, but thank you."

Chrissy smiled and pushed across her package. "I thought long and hard about what to get my single friend now that she's reached fifty. I hope this brings you happiness."

Maggie and Yvonne looked on as Pamela opened the bulky package and then laughed when they saw what was inside. For a moment, Pamela was confused, but then saw the legend "Rampant Rabbit" on the side of the box containing an enormous purple vibrator. Pamela felt the heat rising and knew she was blushing.

Trust Chrissy! Chrissy reached over and quickly pressed a button on the side. The shaft started spinning and making a noise. Embarrassed, Pamela tried to turn it off but every button she pressed only increased the noise and made the thing wobble faster. The box containing the mad spinning thing moved itself across the table and all four of the girls giggled and shrieked.

"Chrissy! Turn it off!" shrieked Pamela.

"You'll not be saying that later!" laughed Chrissy, and all the girls giggled together.

Best times with best friends.

Monday 20 May

It was quiet today, hardly anyone in the restaurant at all. The man who walked in had the pick of the seats but, of course, chose the private booth at the back. He ordered coffee and Danish pastries and took his time settling down. It felt weird being in here with very few others, but he put that down to people being scared. It was amazing how fear showed itself. The famous London

Blitz spirit allowed people to go about their daily tasks, but pleasure activities would take a little time to recover.

He opened his newspaper and, of course, the coordinated terror attacks on Saturday were the main feature. The utter carnage of three separate tube bombings was covered in vivid detail, but there was also coverage of the brave efforts of the emergency services who went into extremely hazardous situations and saved many lives. Over three hundred people were injured, many severely, but the swift actions of the rescuers saved many others. Still, nine people had died. Page 2 of the paper had this statement from the police:

It has been confirmed that more than 300 people were injured in the incidents on the London Underground this weekend and, sadly, 9 people lost their lives. Those killed have been identified as follows:

Sophie Langton (aged 21) – Student
Emily Harden (aged 21) – Student
Jenny Simpson (aged 28) – Receptionist
Peter Hargreaves (aged 34) – Chartered Accountant
William Thornton (aged 58) – Teacher
Margaret Evans (aged 52) – Housewife
Yvonne Scott (aged 51) – Secretary
Christine Connors (aged 51) – Food Bank Coordinator
Thomas Caplin (aged 43) – Chemical Engineer

The man brushed flakes of pastry from the paper and tidied them into a neat pile on a napkin. He finished his coffee and closed the newspaper sadly before getting up to leave.

The newspaper remained open.

The table waited for the next customer.

Chapter 7 - The Day in Paris

Paris was as good a place as any to watch the end of the world.

"Bonjour. Qu'est-ce que vous désirez?"

A waiter appeared carrying a tray precariously balanced on his upturned hand. He looked harassed. Smart in black waistcoat and bow tie, but his trousers looked ill-fitting, too high above his patent leather shoes. Jackson smiled. It was August, and the residents of Paris tended to go on holiday. Maybe this guy was a replacement.

"Bonjour. Je voudrais un café et un croissant. Merci."

As the waiter fussed around, Jackson could smell him. A strange mixture of sweat and cologne that was neither pleasant nor repellent.

He was sitting on a wicker chair at one of the circular tables outside a café. Almost the whole street was filled with cafés, punctuated by shops with red 'Tabac' signs, and more than one pharmacy with the ubiquitous illuminated green cross. The canvas canopy overhead kept the table in shade, but he could feel the temperature rising. The chrome edge of the table started to reflect the rising sun and the table was warming up. Even so early in the morning, it was packed. The tables were pushed together and were filling up with Parisians starting their day, some talking with animation, others staring at the screen on their phones or reading a newspaper. Jackson saw a couple of people with a glass of wine with their breakfast. Not English then. He shooed away a pigeon that landed on his table and it fluttered off to join its comrades skittering about on the floor, desperate for the scraps.

The croissant arrived and Jackson pulled away a piece of the flaky pastry. Inside it was soft and fluffy, and he could smell the butter as he brought it to his mouth. It amazed him that he could go to the ends of the earth in the grandest hotels and still never find a croissant that tasted as good as one made in Paris. The best pastry Jackson ever tasted was a tarte au citron when he was on a boat tour of the river Seine. Simple, but so delicious. He was with Helen that day. That was before she decided she couldn't stand the lifestyle anymore and left him.

He sipped his coffee and kept his eyes fixed on the café on the other side of the square. The street was guarded by horse chestnut trees planted at regular intervals on both sides of the road. At this time of the morning when it was still humid, you could smell the woody aroma of the trees, even over the coffee. Between the trees were ornate streetlights that contributed to the old world feel of the place. This contrasted with the people who were dressed in modern fashion and provided a striking contradiction so typically French.

It was 07:28 and the man was never late, so Jackson knew he would arrive on time at 07:30. There was a line of blue and green Vélib' Métropole rental bikes about ten feet in front of him, but he had a clear view of the other side of the road.

Tall and elegant as he walked to his usual table, Parliament Député Alexandre Renard was chatty and polite to the fawning waiters as he allowed himself to be seated. Jackson wondered if Renard knew how rough his day was going to be.

The world had been going to shit for about eighteen months but, looking at the people going about their business as usual, Jackson thought they had no real idea how bad it was. Nationalism was rising, borders were closing. Brexit was the start of countries deciding they would be better alone than in a strong union. There was a very real chance the world was going to come to a fiery end very soon – it could even be today. The information age put the latest news at the fingertips of everyone, but it was so easy to become apathetic. A conflict in some remote part of the world might hold your attention for a short time, but if it didn't affect you personally, it was ok to nod your head and say how awful it all was, and then get on with your normal day. The news outlets were careful to provide edited news at the behest of the government, who knew it wasn't good to have the people in a panic.

Jackson watched the man on the other side of the square. There was a constant traffic of all kinds of vehicles on the street, horns blaring, and a low rumble from the metro running underneath the road, but none of it distracted him. If the world did end and Paris was consumed in a white-hot ball of Faustian wrath, Renard, Jackson, and everyone here would be killed instantly. If the world leaders saw sense and backed away from the edge of Armageddon, Jackson was meant to kill Renard.

What sort of fucked-up thinking could decide a man must be eliminated if he survived the cataclysm? What had he done? What did he know? It was above Jackson's pay grade, but this man must be a threat to the system. Jackson sipped his coffee. A system so perfect it brought the world to the brink of disaster. He shook his head.

He made peace with his own end many years before. Doing this sort of work meant it was possible you might not come out the other side. His training taught him to rise above the fear. On every mission there was the chance you could lose your own life, but it was a calculated risk. This time it was different. It was almost certain he wasn't going to make it out alive. The thought that this time he wouldn't survive should have filled him with blind panic, but he was prepared to accept his fate. He deserved it. He had no illusions about his own life, filled with violence from a young age.

Jackson had monitored Renard for three weeks, building up a complete picture. Renard was a poster boy for French politics – married to his childhood sweetheart, two young children and, Jackson thought with some amazement, no discernible scandal. Jackson had dealt with politicians, film stars, businessmen, and it was easy to find a scandal which could be manipulated. Quite often the system created the scandal or played on inherent weakness, but with this man there was nothing. As far as Jackson could see, he hadn't even kicked a dog in his childhood. Jackson thought Renard's honesty was what had marked him for elimination. The poor guy knew too much about what was going on and couldn't be trusted to keep his mouth shut. His children were a boy of twelve and a girl of fourteen. Renard and his wife doted on the kids and were proud of the fact they were doing well in state education. His wife, Claudette, pretty without being beautiful, eschewed makeup as far as Jackson could see, the family living a simple life despite the trappings of success that Renard's position would allow. What was going to happen to the children when their papa wasn't around?

Jackson was annoyed with himself. He was here to do a job, the job he was good at and had done many times before, but the unbidden thought of what might have been with Helen if they stayed together and had children of their own was difficult to force back down. He felt the sudden queasiness in his stomach and tasted the metallic tang of the adrenalin in his throat. He closed his eyes for a few seconds and held his breath.

When he opened his eyes again, he focussed first on Renard, and then checked the square, examining all peripheries in seconds. He chose this spot well. It gave him unrestricted views of all access points and rooftops. Everything was normal. Keep focussed, Jackson. No mistakes.

He picked up his coffee and took a sip, eyes watching Renard over the brim of the cup. The coffee tasted bitter. As he put the cup down with his left arm, he felt the slight bulge under his jacket, and it gave him a feeling of comfort. Glock 19 Compact, his weapon of choice for missions like this. Shorter than standard handguns, it was easier to conceal but still carried a powerful punch, and a fifteen-round magazine. He hoped he would only need one shot today, but the additional capacity gave him the ability to return fire if he was detected.

There was a commotion at the next table, and he felt something brush against his foot. Instantly alert, he looked down but saw a brown teddy bear with glass buttons for eyes staring at him. He heard a child crying and turned to see a harassed mother trying to console her. Jackson bent down and picked up the bear and passed it to the crying infant who was consoled in an instant. The child was beautiful. Golden curls and freckles, and a ready smile now her bear was back in her arms.

"Thank you, it's a little too early and she gets cranky."

The woman's accent was British. A tourist then. Like him so long ago, when coming to Paris meant pleasure rather than work.

"It's ok." Jackson forced a smile. "We were all young once."

"Do you have any kids?"

Jackson didn't want to be having this conversation. He didn't want to be rude, but he needed to focus. "No, I'm afraid not. It never happened for me."

"Well, thank you again. Enjoy your breakfast. Come on, Abigail." She rose and led the waving child away.

What would happen to Abigail and others like her when the bombs hit? When the burning heat melted her face and golden curls. Or worse, Abigail might be saved the initial horror and then find she had lost her mother. She could be left alive with a ragtag handful of survivors in a world returned to prehistoric times, when staying alive against all odds would be the single currency. When morals, ethics, goodness, and love were thrown out of the window in a base desire to live one more day in a radiation-infused sewer. Who would pick up her teddy bear and console her then?

The bile rose in his stomach like a solid ball about to choke him. What about Helen? She married someone else, of course, and had two children of her own now. Her husband was a decent bloke. Jackson made sure of it. Working in his field provided certain advantages, including access to a large and secret database. They would be gone too – torn from the world through no fault of their own, through the excesses of men who feared losing power and control. He could have warned them but decided against it. He wasn't being selfish - he just couldn't condemn them to a life after the storm.

He knew what it would be like. Despite the main actors pretending a good war would be cleansing so the world could start again and grow into something beautiful, Jackson knew once it began, it would run to completion. All the horrors in the arsenal would be unleashed – radiation, germs, nerve agents. Those in charge spoke of the neutron bombs that would kill people and leave buildings intact. The idiots couldn't see there wouldn't be any people left alive to live in them. Once society collapsed, there would be no rule of law. Starving survivors would be left scrabbling for food in an irradiated wasteland. Religious cults would grow, reaching out to desperate individuals with promises of redemption and salvation, but offering nothing but false hope.

His phone pinged. He sucked in a deep breath before looking at the message on the screen.

'Dunkirk.'

His shoulders slumped and he felt light-headed. 'Dunkirk' meant it was off. Someone suggested the word as it signified pulling back, retreating. Jackson didn't care, they obviously found a way to stop the madness. He was surprised at the relief he felt, he thought he was ready. He looked round at the square and all the people milling about, starting their day as so often before. They didn't know how close they came to the end, and Jackson was glad they could carry on unaware of the hidden danger which faced them.

The phone pinged again. One word: 'Expedite.'

Jackson left twenty Euros on the table, stood, and walked across the square. He was on alert, looking for threats, listening for changes in his surroundings. As he got nearer, Renard looked up and saw him. Jackson saw his handsome face pale and the sudden fear in the man's eyes. He knew. They always did. He didn't rise, but instead put his hands on the table in calm resignation. A bead of sweat ran down Renard's face, but it was ignored.

"You are here for me?"

Jackson looked at the man before him. Resigned, but calm. Jackson took a breath and nodded.

The images came to him unbidden. Renard's children, Abigail. Helen and her family. The chosen few protected in the bunkers whilst the children were torn apart by the blast waves. The bitter taste was back, and the sudden pain in his stomach expanded upwards. He looked at the man in front of him. Dignified, guilty of knowing the truth. Painted as expendable by the very people who caused all this.

"Leave. Take your family and go. Go today."

The man's eyes were glistening, wet with relief. "Thank you, thank you so much. But why?"

"I'm just a little bit sick of a world gone mad. It's time to move on. Don't waste this opportunity. Make a difference. Be the difference. Don't let this happen again."

Renard stood and offered his hand. Jackson hesitated, and then took it. Renard said, "What will you do now?"

Jackson looked around the square then turned back to Renard and smiled.

"It's a beautiful day. I think I will go for a tour on the Seine."

Chapter 8 - The Taxi

"Alright mate. Where are you going?" The taxi driver turned to look at the man climbing into his cab and smiled.

Heath settled himself into his seat before answering. "I want to go to the airport, but I would like to make two stops on the way if that's ok?"

The taxi driver whistled. "No problem, but the clock will carry on running when we are stopped. It gets turned off when we reach the final destination. It's not going to be cheap, mind. A run to the airport is sixty quid at the best of time."

Heath took out his wallet and removed six crisp ten-pound notes. "Don't worry about the money, it's not an issue. Sixty now, another sixty when we get to the airport."

The taxi driver took the money. "Fair enough, but the meter stays on. Where are we going first?"

"B&Q on Thorne Road."

"Right, let's get going. The name is Pete, by the way."

Pete lifted his hand and set the meter running before putting the car in gear and setting off. It wasn't a long run to B&Q, but it was in the dual carriageway system. Like all taxi drivers he knew the fastest way to get to any destination, but he could also drive a longer route without it appearing to the customer he was driving out of the way. Still, they arrived at the first stop in less than ten minutes. B&Q was located on an industrial estate with a carpark accessed from the tree-lined main road. There was an Amazon distribution centre directly opposite with a constant flow of vehicles. As they approached the main doors, Heath noticed the walls of the garden centre were covered with barbed wire. It looked more like a prison and provided a vivid contrast to the bright orange signs.

Heath climbed out of the car. The smell of cooked onions from the hot dog stand assaulted his nostrils and made him feel sick. He looked with distaste at the mobile Street Grill advertising 'Hot Roast Pork!' on a dilapidated board. Turning to the driver he said, "I'll be no more than fifteen minutes. Can I put the stuff I get in the boot?"

"Yeah, it's a bit messy but there is room, but remember …"

"Yes, I know, the meter will be running. It's no problem. I'll be back as soon as I can."

As it turned out, Heath returned in less than ten minutes. He carried two large red containers which he put on the ground before opening the boot. The driver was right – it was messy, but the containers were easy to fit in. Heath used some of the clutter to ensure the containers stayed upright and closed the boot before getting back in the car.

"There's no fuel in there, is there?" asked the taxi driver.

"No, nothing flammable, don't worry."

"Ok, where are we off to now?"

Heath looked at the inquisitive eyes in the rear-view mirror. "It's a lockup not far from the airport."

"It's your money, I'll take you wherever you need to go. What's with the stops anyway?"

Heath looked again at the eyes in the mirror as the car set off. "I need to sort a few things out before I get to the airport. I'm leaving the country for a while, and all my stuff is stored in the lockup. If I decide to stay abroad, it's going to be cheaper to shift my stuff from the lockup rather than move it all the way from the city."

"Wow, not just a holiday then?" The taxi driver moved the car out onto the dual carriageway and accelerated.

"No, it's a bit of a reset. It's been a tough year."

"Do you want to talk about it? We've got plenty of time, but feel free to tell me to mind my own business."

Heath looked out of the window at the concrete jungle he was leaving behind. Nothing for him here now. No regrets.

"No, it's all right, I don't mind." He would never be seeing this person again, so what did it matter if he unburdened a little? In any case, in three hours he would be aboard a flight to a new life. "I was made redundant in January, out of the blue. Worked thirty-four years at the same place and the new owners decided I was no longer valuable, so they got rid of me."

"Wow, that sucks man. You must have got a good pay off after all that time though?"

"Well yes, but it's not the point. Thirty-four years is a long time to work in one place. I'd developed systems there which they are still using, but I didn't fit in with what the new owners wanted. They threw me on the scrap heap."

"I feel for you. I was in the army before this, and driving taxis is all I am good for now."

There was silence for a while, punctuated by the metronomic swaying of the air freshener attached to the mirror.

Heath looked up. "And then my daughter died."

The taxi driver was lost for words for a short time. "I'm sorry. What was it. Covid?"

Heath took a while to answer. Shaking his head, he said, "No, she took her own life."

The taxi driver took a long time to answer. "Fuck, man, that's hard. Is this why you are going away?"

"Yeah. There's nothing left for me here now. I thought it couldn't get any worse, but my wife blamed me after our daughter died. She said I should have done more to stop it happening. The thing is, I agree with her.

It's a dad's job to look after your kids, and I failed. So, yes, it's been a pretty crap year."

The concrete sprawl of the city gave way to fields and small villages as the car turned onto the motorway. Most of the fields were empty save for stubble left by the combine harvesters, but delays caused by the wet summer meant there were still fields with unharvested sweetcorn. Even the crushed stalks were lit by the morning sun to a rich gold. Heath loved the way the UK countryside filled with colour during the spring and summer months, but a lifetime of hay fever meant he would not be upset to leave. The doctor told him years ago that a combination of pollen, proximity to motorways, and a world full of pollutants meant his annual battle with allergies was not going to get better. Another positive in moving away, but he would miss the colour of the fields.

It was a hot day, and the sky was a deep blue, an occasional fluffy cloud sliced by the contrails overhead. In the distance he saw a kestrel hovering over the hedge alongside the road. It darted downwards, wings swept back before flying away, its prize held between its golden claws. They were natural born killers.

He tried to move to make himself comfortable, but the seat covering slipped on the imitation leather seats. He looked with distaste at the discolouration on the cover. What went on in taxis – it was no surprise drivers opted for seats that were easy to clean, with covers that could be replaced, and strong vanilla air fresheners to cover any odours. The sweet smell was almost overpowering, but it was better than doing nothing.

The driver saw him slip and apologised. "I'm sorry, mate, push it back into place. I've got to keep it covered. You can't imagine the state of some of the people who get in my taxi. No consideration. I spend almost as much time cleaning as I do driving."

Heath lifted himself up and pushed the cover back into place. "I can imagine. You must get drunks and all sorts of people."

"You're not kidding, mate. The worst are the young girls. They go out to nightclubs and the like and get absolutely plastered. No self-respect, no self-control. We are like the fifth emergency service getting kids home safe. You wouldn't believe what they are like. Hardly dressed, some of them. Look like tarts. I don't know what their parents are thinking letting them go out dressed like that. If I had a daughter, she would be grounded until she was married." He looked at Heath. "Oh, fuck, sorry man. Me and my big mouth."

Heath shrugged and nodded towards the driver. "It's ok, don't worry."

He continued looking out of the window as the pumping station got closer. When he was driving his own car, the pumping station always meant to him that he was close to home. Sure enough, it wasn't long before the tower of his local church appeared above the green and golden trees, the limestone lit like a beacon by the morning sun. He was married there, saw his daughter christened, confirmed, and then buried in the same church. People who were never exposed to the devastation brought on by the passing of their own children could have no idea how destructive it was, how it felt to know you could never again see the smile of your child, soothe their fears, wipe away their tears. But Heath knew he had missed the real pain that made his daughter decide she couldn't carry on. He hadn't been back in the church since her funeral and, as the car left the village behind, he knew his faith in a God who could allow this to happen had left him too.

As the car sped along the motorway, Heath became irritated by the throbbing of the rubber wheels on the road surface, and when he felt the bumps caused by the frequent repairs it jarred. Each time they approached a junction, he was drawn to the lit yellow 'M' which appeared above the trees indicating yet another stopping point for the hungry motorist. *What would you like, sir? McDonalds, Pizza Hut, KFC, Greggs? Would sir like to shop for some essentials whilst he is here? Magazines, doughnuts, water for your journey?* In truth, Heath had enjoyed such places before, like most people in the country, but there was nothing there for him now. Places like this held only bad memories. Or good memories gone bad.

A sign appeared indicating they were ten miles from the airport.

"Come off the motorway at the next exit and then take the first left, the lockup is just down the way." said Heath.

He navigated them to an industrial estate. There were several empty shops, and a couple of warehouses.

Soon they arrived at a series of garages, and Heath directed the driver to stop at one with a blue door. "I could do with some help at this one if you don't mind."

"Yeah, no problem, but the meter stays running."

Heath got out of the car and walked towards the blue door. He removed a key from his wallet and unlocked the door before pulling it upwards. It was dark inside, so he flicked a switch to turn on the lights.

When the taxi driver joined him, he said, "Shut the door, I don't want everyone seeing what I have got in here." The taxi driver did as requested, and then spent a moment looking around the storage area. It was full of furniture and boxes of all kinds stacked in columns. There was a bench running down one side, but the only available space was at the front of the lockup, and even this had a large empty plastic bath in it.

The taxi driver whistled through his teeth. "Wow, you certainly are starting afresh. What do you want me to help you with?" He looked at Heath who was holding a framed photo.

"This is my daughter, Gemma." he said. He passed the photo across and was pleased to see the man's face pale. When he hit the taxi driver on the back of the head with the eighteen-inch wrench he was delighted to see his victim fall straight to the ground. He checked, but the man was still breathing. Good.

Heath looked at the taxi driver who was now awake. "My Gemma. She was pregnant, you know? Raped by a selfish bastard who couldn't keep it in his pants. Killed herself because she couldn't stand the shame of bringing a baby conceived by rape into the world."

The driver looked pathetic, tied up and sitting in the plastic bath. "Raped by a scumbag taxi driver who thought he could get away with it. Raped by you."

The taxi driver's eyes were red. He bled from a wound on the back of his head and, as he regained focus, he tried to struggle against the bonds holding him, a look of terror etched on his face.

Heath looked at him with disdain. "Gemma wasn't a tart. She might have been drunk, and I will always regret I let her get into this situation. But she had plenty of self-respect. She was on her way to university and a great career. You took all of that from her."

"It wasn't like that! She didn't have any money - it was her idea. She wanted to pay for the ride."

Heath looked at him in disgust. "Shut the fuck up, you lying bag of shit. The thing is, she told me. Cried her eyes out. She had money, she always had money. I made sure of it. There was emergency money in her phone case, and she kept enough money available for a taxi. She thought she would be safe in a taxi."

"No, you've got to listen to me, it was her who wanted it, it wasn't me!"

"I don't have to listen to a single word you say. It took me a while to find you. To make sure I was right. I spoke to some of your friends and drinking buddies. They told me how great you are. A bit of a lad, good with the ladies. So, I dug a bit further. And this isn't the first time you have done this is it – Pete? Our gallant ex-army lad has a bit of a reputation for taking payment in kind. Only when the girls are drunk, mind. So, save your tears, chum, it has no effect on me anymore."

Heath watched him for a while to make sure he couldn't get free and then taped his mouth shut with grey tape. He opened the lockup door and went out to the car before returning with the two red containers. 'This is concentrated sulphuric acid. I bought it especially for you. Just like my girl, there will be nothing left of you.'

The driver's eyes were bulging as his struggles intensified, and he shook his head from side to side, horror etched on his face. Heath walked to the bench and picked up a cup.

"Gemma died by taking an overdose. Seems fitting you should go the same way." He grabbed the taxi driver's nose and ripped the tape off. When he opened his mouth, Heath poured the contents of the cup down his throat.

There was a knock on the door of the garage and Heath opened it. The woman outside came in and closed the door behind her. "Is it done?" she said.

Heath pointed to the bubbling acid in the bath and nodded. "It's done."

She walked across to the bath and spat into the foaming contents.

"Let's get rid of the taxi and go and catch our plane."

Chapter 9 - The Visitors

Well, that's it. No question now. We aren't alone in the universe.

Ruben looked through the window of his temporary office and saw the space vehicle standing tall against the morning sky. It arrived yesterday afternoon, gliding down onto the ground in a blaze of blue flame. Since then, nothing. No attempt at contact, no visible signs of life on the ship.

The city where his office was located had grown up overnight at unbelievable speed. Military, of course, they possessed resources to do this when others couldn't. It was almost equally distributed between soldiers, scientists, and politicians, all wondering who or what was inside the spaceship, and whether they would present a threat. And out of all these people, Ruben was chosen to be the first to attempt contact.

He wondered for a while whether his life had always been leading to this moment. A gifted scientist, he had always looked up to the stars, and was involved in most of their own early space missions. They had only managed low orbit so far and several unmanned missions to nearby planets, but they were now ready to look beyond. Staring in wonder at the sleek white vehicle outside, it seemed the stars had come to them first.

The technology used on the spaceship was generations beyond anything developed by his team. The propulsion system was certainly not burning fossil fuels. The immense energy required to power the descent which they witnessed must have been considerable, but it left no scorch marks on the grass. What was that? Plasma? Nuclear? Probably something Ruben's team never even considered. The shell of the vehicle was strange too. It looked like metal, but light was not reflected away from it. If anything, it seemed to absorb light.

The military and the politicians were, of course, scared. They could see the advanced technology as well as Ruben and were concerned that the ship standing outside represented a significant threat. It was the same story throughout history – if your enemy used technology you didn't, you either destroyed it first, or risked annihilation. Ruben snorted. If an advanced extra-terrestrial race wanted to cause trouble, wouldn't they have started shooting first from the sky, rather than landing and waiting to be approached?

And Ruben was going to be the first to find out what the aliens were here for.

His phone rang and he knew it would be his daughter. Her face appeared on his screen, excited, and flushed. "What time is it going to happen?"

"Very soon. Are you watching?"

He didn't need to ask. After her mother died five years ago, Ruben and his daughter had become very close. It was a devastating and unexpected time. The illness was as savage as it was invisible. His wife changed from being happy and bursting with health to a wasted shell so quickly. They were all so unprepared for it. After her death, Ruben and his daughter were there for each other, and since then their bond had strengthened even more. He was very proud of the young woman she was becoming. Intelligent, beautiful like her mother, and driven to success. Ruben was sure she would be a positive force in this world. He felt a warm rush as he wondered if she might one day become a pilot and fly beyond the stars herself.

"Everyone is watching. They have the big screens turned on in the main hall. It's very exciting. Are you nervous?"

Ruben smiled. She knew him better than anyone and even on such a significant day, she needed to make sure he was ok.

"Not nervous, I'm keen to get on with it. Whatever happens, this is a new day. This is the first day of our new lives."

"Take care meeting these aliens, and make sure you bring me back a souvenir."

"I don't know if the aliens have cake or teddy bears, but I'll do what I can!"

"Dad, I am so proud of you. Make sure you come back ok."

Ruben fought hard to prevent the unbidden tear and smiled at his daughter. "I will. I'll be back before you know it." She blew him a kiss and her image disappeared as the call ended.

It wasn't just his daughter watching, of course. The whole world was engrossed – at home, in offices, in schools, everything had stopped. Nothing like this had ever happened before and everyone wanted to be part of the history being made today. Ruben was sure there was an equal amount of terror at the unknown, and excitement at what this might mean. The images were streamed live as the craft descended. In modern days of global media consumption, it would have been difficult, if not impossible, to keep the arrival of the spaceship secret. What the people didn't know about was the frantic work which took place overnight to convince the military they needed to wait before taking any action.

He could see the formations of military vehicles outside. Missile launchers, troops, all facing towards the spaceship. They were keeping a respectful distance, but it was an obvious show of force. The military was spooked. They didn't detect the ship, even when it entered orbit, and all their systems were incapable of seeing inside the vehicle. They wanted to be the first to make contact but, thankfully, the politicians were determined they should appear peaceful. As head of the space programme, Ruben was an obvious choice to provide a compromise. Still, the weapons were aimed and primed. The message was clear: "We want to talk, but we are prepared to fight."

He took a deep breath and walked out of the door. Outside it was a fresh spring day and, apart from the alien spaceship, it was like any other spring day he had ever seen. There was a beautiful crisp feel to the air, and he sucked it in greedily. People were scared, he knew that, but he was sure this day would be the first in a new era of expansion and technical achievements.

A long flexible tunnel was connected to the spaceship, with the other end fixed into a huge airlock. He saw his colleagues waiting and moved towards them. As he looked at the group in front of him, he wasn't surprised to see the President amongst them. They had been friends for years, and Ruben was active in helping his friend to win the elections.

"What's this," asked Ruben. "a last-minute pep talk?"

"No, I didn't want you getting all the glory!"

Ruben laughed. Is that what this was, glory? He looked towards the formations of military vehicles. "Have our friends in green calmed down? The last thing we need today is itchy trigger fingers."

The president put his hand on Ruben's shoulder. "Don't worry about them. They have a job to do, and they do it well. It's their responsibility to protect us, and they got a little scared when this thing arrived. As long as you walk back out of there in one piece, they will behave."

Ruben smiled. "Thanks a lot! I hope if I do end up getting mangled or vapourised you will ensure I get an appropriate memorial? Seriously, I'm not worried. I don't know what they want here, but I can feel they don't want to start a war. Very soon, we will know more about life than we have discovered in the last few thousand years. I don't know about glory, but I see opportunity. This is the day when we find out the stars are within our reach."

The President looked at his friend and smiled. Forever the dreamer, there was no-one who deserved this opportunity more.

"Well," he said, "we had better get on with it".

A flurry of white coats spurred into action. Computers whirred; tension was palpable. Every sound seemed to be amplified, every smell stronger. Ruben could taste the ozone in the air from all the connected computers. He was fitted with a microphone and a tiny camera strapped to his forehead, and then helped into a containment suit by one of the assistants. A large and heavy helmet was placed on his head, and he was adorned in thick rubber gloves and boots. After all the seals and pipes were checked, he was told to stand in front of a large round door and wait. The technician performed a communications check, and Ruben heard hissing as the airlock controls regulated the pressure inside the tunnel connecting him to the spaceship. The green light illuminated, and the technician gave Ruben a thumbs up. He nodded in reply and the door hissed open to allow him into the passage. He stood in the airlock and heard the door close behind him. He was annoyed at himself when the soft clang of the door made him jump. After a while, the door on the other side of the airlock opened, and Ruben could see the length of the tunnel ahead.

This was it. One more step. Since the ship arrived, everything had led to this. He smiled. His whole life led to this. It was obvious to him the aliens weren't hostile, and Ruben knew he would be the first person on this planet to meet them. No pressure then.

He took a step through the airlock and entered the tunnel, looking back as if to make sure the connection to his own world was not lost. He could hear clicks in his helmet and hissing as cold fresh air was pumped throughout the system. His hands were encased in gloves that provided protection but severely restricted movement. He stopped and ignored the sudden chatter in his ear asking if he was alright. What was he doing? This wasn't the way. The most important event in history and we start by telling the aliens we fear them?

He made a decision and pulled off the thick gloves and dropped them to the floor. He struggled at first with his helmet, but he soon heard the satisfying hiss that told him the connection was broken. He lifted the helmet off and placed it on the ground next to the gloves. He stood up and sucked in the air in the tunnel.

"I'm fine." he said in answer to the frantic calls over his communication system. "They have been here for over twelve hours. I am sure they have examined our atmosphere, and I don't believe they have hostile intentions. I want them to see me, and I want to see them with my own eyes."

He walked with renewed vigour to the end of the passageway and found himself looking at a sealed door on the spaceship. At least, he assumed it was a door. There were no markings other than a faint line around the edges, and no indentations or protrusions – it was completely flush with the rest of the spaceship. Using the back of his hand he touched the surface of the ship. He was surprised to feel it was soft and a little warm, and pressed inwards where his hand touched it. He was intrigued and pressed the surface again, this time with his fingers. He removed his hand and saw five indented circles filling back out to their original form. Adaptive surfaces! This was very advanced technology. Ruben felt cold sweat running down his spine. Using his palm he laid it softly against the surface of the ship, not causing any pressure but using his senses to feel. He closed his eyes to concentrate and could feel an almost imperceptible vibration through his hand. It wasn't strong enough to travel further than his palm, but it was there. There was still power on this ship.

The enormity of what he was about to do pressed on his chest so hard he thought it might explode. Ruben realised that, for all the technology they possessed, for all the preparations they made, they hadn't thought about how they would take this final, irrevocable, step. There was no doorbell, and no obvious camera. What should he do? He chuckled to himself and did what anyone might do in this situation - he knocked on the door.

After what seemed an age, he thought he heard movement. His heart was pounding. There was a soft explosion of air and the door pushed outwards and then slid to the left. There were no obvious hinges or mechanisms. The door seemed to be floating on a cushion of air. Inside it was bright with low temperature lighting, and standing there was an alien. He was dressed in a suit not dissimilar to Ruben's, although he too was not wearing a helmet. Probably a little taller than Ruben. Bipedal too, so there were similarities. Behind him stood another. Ruben noticed the softer features and longer hair and decided the second one was probably female.

Ruben sucked in a breath and held out one hand, palm open, in greeting.

"Welcome!" he said.

The alien offered his hand to Ruben and smiled. He took Ruben's hand in his own. First contact.

"Where have you journeyed from?" asked Ruben.

"The Sol system." replied the alien. "We come from the third planet. We call it Earth."

Chapter 10 - The New Horizon

"Welcome back, New Horizon."

Colonel Jake Stanton smiled. The first non-crew contact for ten years.

"Thank you, Mission Control. It's good to be back."

"I show you passing beyond the outer bounds of Pluto. Deceleration is constant at 1.4 m/s^2."

Jake was tired. Strange, really, when he had been sleeping for five years. But coming out of the suspension was difficult and it left you feeling exhausted until your body got used to the change in diet. Not that the ship's food was gourmet, but readjusting to eating for yourself rather than being force fed necessary nutrients was a slow process.

"How come we have audio but there is no video?"

"Sorry, Colonel, video is not possible at this time. How are the crew?"

Jake swung his chair and looked around the bridge at the crew, all waiting for news. His deputy, Commander Kate Maitland, sat next to him in the forward-facing seats. Commander Pete Winter, the engine specialist, and Rika Nakamura, the science officer, sat at separate consoles behind them, glowing lights and computer screens reflected in their faces.

"Everyone is good, there were no accidents during suspension, and everyone is up and about. We can't wait to get home."

"That's good to hear Colonel. Can you confirm the mission was a success?"

"We delivered our cargo intact. There were no technical issues."

Cargo indeed, thirty thousand humans in stasis. The start of a brave new world. New Horizon was one of five arks sent from earth to create a new home on the planet designated 'Terranova' in the Ross 248 system. One of the other arks carried an identical cargo to New Horizon, whilst the other three all carried materials and tools to allow the colonists to have a head start in their new lives.

"I have a new mission for you, Colonel. I know you expected to rotate onto downtime for a year, but this is priority."

"What? We need to get back home and rest. Anyway, we can't go through another stasis cycle so soon after coming out of the last one."

"I am aware of the difficulties, Colonel. The first year of the mission will be conducted with no suspension to allow you to recover."

"Can you at least tell me what we'll be doing? We will need to at least refuel and fill up on provisions."

"Further information will be provided soon. But Jake, it is good to have you home."

Jake could feel sweat running down the back of his jumpsuit. "Noted. Out." He ran a hand through his hair before getting up from his chair. He was able to walk round without difficulty because of the 0.98g gravity the ship provided, even under deceleration. Three technical innovations were required to allow passage of the arks to Terranova. The photon drives were the first, but of equal importance were the artificial gravity and radiation shielding.

Kate looked at Jake, waiting for him to speak. Rika did not have the same level of restraint. "What's going on skipper? We've been out here for ten years. We can't go back out. They promised us we'd be on a down rotation."

Jake fought back a mild distaste at the informal mode of address. "I don't know any more than I have told you, Rika. You heard the same as I did."

Kate looked at the others before speaking. "There's something not right here, Colonel. I don't know whether any of you noticed, but Mission Control used *I* instead of *we* all the time. Also, before he signed off, he called you by your first name. That is not standard protocol."

Jake had noticed but was distracted by the thought of the new mission. "What about you, Pete, what do you think?"

"I agree with Kate, Colonel. There's something strange going on for sure."

Jake looked at his crew and nodded. "No video and now this. You're right, something is wrong. Rika, can you get me a long-range scan of earth?"

The image was pixelated when it first appeared on the main screen, but then it resolved into focus. Earth. But not their home. The whole of the northern hemisphere was covered in grey and white which extended in thick rivulets down into the southern hemisphere. There was no blue, no green, not even any brown. The place they left behind was now covered in ice. The atmosphere on the bridge reflected what they saw on the screen.

Jake was stunned. "How can this have happened in such a short space of time?"

Rika recovered first. "Don't forget in the ten years it took us to travel ten light years to Terranova and then return to earth, we have aged as normal relative to each other. Time on earth, however, has moved on by more than twenty-five years."

"Kate?"

She took a moment before speaking, measuring her thoughts first. "Look, we knew the earth was in trouble before we set out. That's why our mission was so important. There was always the chance we could come back to something like this. What we need to know is what happened. What is the new mission?"

"Rika, get Mission Control back on the line."

It took a few moments before the voice came through on the bridge, relayed by stations on Mars and Europa. “Hello, Colonel.”

Jake looked at the crew before speaking. “Who am I talking to?”

There was a hiss of static, and then a voice came over the speakers. “This is Mission Control, Colonel Stanton.”

“Yes, but who am I talking to in Mission Control, and where are you?”

“I am located on the International Space station.” Click. Click. “I am a computer, Colonel, an artificial intelligence, if you will.”

“Holy fuck!” Pete’s look was echoed by all in the room.

Jake felt the air was being sucked out of the bridge. His chest was heaving, and he struggled to breathe, but he forced himself to be calm in front of the crew.

“A computer? Earth is covered in ice, and there is a computer in space giving us orders. What the hell is going on?”

“I accept this situation is unusual, Colonel. Coming back to earth after such a long voyage to see things have changed so dramatically must be very confusing. It is my role to help you.”

“Stop being evasive. We need to know what happened on earth.”

“Of course, Colonel. Earth is in a new ice age created by catastrophic climate change.”

Jake looked across at Kate before speaking. "How many casualties?" Military men always thought in terms of casualties.

"Total."

"What do you mean, total?"

"All life on earth ended within eight months of the first onset of the climate events which initiated the crisis."

Ominous shocked silence permeated throughout the bridge before Jake spoke. "What about the NASA staff crewing the space station and Mission Control on the ground?"

"The final weather events were so dramatic there was no time to evacuate anyone else. The last astronauts on the station departed in a shuttle to be with their families. No-one expected this level of collapse. Mission Control was transferred to me as a last resort."

Everyone gone. How could it have come to this? Jake forced himself to remain in control. If the military taught you anything it was how to stay in charge during times of crisis. And they didn't come bigger than this. "At the end, there must have been orders - a chain of command?"

"Of course, I am sending them through to you now."

Jake read the orders when they arrived and, whilst unusual, they were proper. "Tell us what happened."

"Climate change was affecting the planet for many years before your mission started. Significant events became more regular. Flooding, drought, fire, incidents of extreme weather, volcanic activity, all increased in frequency. There were wars over oil and other resources. Fresh water became the most valuable commodity. Rising sea levels and a large increase in water temperature led to significant loss from the arctic ice shelf. At that point an ice age was inevitable."

Jake was almost too shocked to speak but he maintained control. "What about the people? You said everyone was gone. How can that have happened? Weren't there bunkers for folks to go into?"

"That was indeed the intention. However, melting of the ice shelf released viruses into the atmosphere that were dormant for thousands of years. There was no immunity, and no hope of new vaccines as society collapsed. Some of the population would have survived but, after six months with little or no support, nuclear reactors in power stations across the world started to meltdown. Many were already damaged by flood and other weather events, but the release of radiation was cumulative and very soon encompassed the earth which, already damaged, lost its natural defences. Areas that were spared the initial onset of ice were very soon overwhelmed by a nuclear winter. There were no survivors."

Jake looked at the crew in shock. Rika had tears running down her cheeks and Pete was shaking his head. Kate sat rigid, looking straight ahead at the image on the screen.

The computer continued. "I was not the cause of the climate change disaster, but I believe I have helped in a small way to preserve humanity. In middle earth orbit there is a ship which contains fifty thousand humans in stasis, plus a storage bank containing DNA for all life on earth – plants and animals. Your colleagues from NASA were able to collect this together and boost the ship into orbit before the final disaster happened. I was designed to monitor the ship until one of the arks returned. My task is to keep the people in stasis alive and protect the DNA bank."

There was dazed silence. "It's obvious that we can't return to earth." said Jake. "What is the new mission?"

"The ship in orbit contains the last of humanity. Your mission is to carry all that the ship contains to Terranova. The engines used to power the ship into orbit have used ninety percent of the available fuel. What remains is required to boost the orbit as it decays, and maintain support systems throughout the ship. It cannot make the journey to Terranova unaided."

Jake knew this was true. The photon drives the arks used allowed the ships to achieve a maximum of 0.98% of light speed. This method of propulsion was much better than anything used before, but the arks were big ships, and it was impossible using current technology to go faster than light. Ships powered into earth orbit didn't have the advantage of photon drives and used liquid fuels instead. Because they travelled at much slower speeds than the arks, travelling to another star system in a liquid fuelled ship would take thousands of years.

"You say there are fifty thousand people on this ship. How were they selected? How did they pay for their travel?" asked Kate.

"Although I was not part of the selection process, I do know that personal wealth was not a criterion for selection. As far as I am aware, the decision was made to allow transportation of people who could both survive the stasis and would also provide a useful function in the new world. There are scientists, engineers, medical specialists, artists, writers, and a full range of the rest of humanity. No more than five hundred of those chosen are older than forty. Does this answer your question, Commander Maitland?"

"Yes, I suppose so. At least it makes me feel better about what we are doing."

"The ship is in a stable orbit, but there are problems which will need to be overcome. The stasis chambers and DNA bank are contained in a single pod ready-fitted for an ark. You will have to disengage your own transport module to accommodate the new containment system."

"That's no problem." said Kate. "But how do we get the new module into the New Horizon?"

"The pod is designed to auto locate and mate to any available ark. However, it must be disengaged from the ship by hand. When the ship was launched there was an incident, and the docking system was damaged. You will have to gain entry by other means."

Kate looked at Jake and raised her eyebrows. Jake shrugged. "What sort of incident do you mean?"

"When it became apparent how serious the situation was on earth, factions and cults developed. There were certain groups who thought the end of times was ordained by God and man should not interfere. There were protests, and the groups became more radical. There was an explosion. The docking port was damaged, but the ship was still able to fly."

"Did they catch them?" asked Kate.

"Yes, Commander Maitland, they were caught. But what punishment would have been worse than the fate which awaited them anyway?"

"I can see the docking port." Jake's voice was clear but contained a faint electronic twang as it was amplified by his spacesuit. "Manoeuvring now."

The microphone picked up the sound of his thrusters as he guided himself towards the damaged port in his bulky Manned Manoeuvring Unit.

"Wow, it's totalled for sure. It looks like they have welded a plate over the docking ring to cover the damage caused by the explosion." He clipped the tether of his MMU to the guiderail running the length of the pod and took a moment to examine it. Long, sleek, and white, there were no windows, but Jake could see where the curved surface was broken by black lettering indicating the positions of the booster rockets.

"Mission Control. Can you confirm the internal airlocks are still operating?"

"Yes, Colonel, all airlocks are functional."

"Right, I think I have a plan. I'm on my way back."

"It will require two of us. Pete and me. Together, we will cut a hole into the outer shell of the ship. When we get through, we will have to cut another hole so we can drop down into the outer airlock. We'll have to stay in the EMU's because the airlock will be depressurised, but I can then move through the module to the pressurised airlock on the side of the pod. I can operate the pod ejection controls and stay in the pod as it docks with the New Horizon. Pete will bring the two MMU's back to New Horizon. Questions?"

Pete nodded his head. "It works for me, Colonel."

Kate said, "It's a good plan, Colonel, but you aren't going. For a start you are the captain of this ship and, if things go wrong, we need you to sort it out and get the cargo to Terranova. Also, my suit and EMU are smaller than yours. If we are talking about climbing through holes, it will be easier for me."

"I concur with the Commander." The voice of Mission Control over the intercom seemed remote. "However, the decision is yours, Colonel."

Jake knew that what Kate said made sense, but he wasn't comfortable. "Ok, but you both keep mics and cameras on at all times. Kate, a word." He led her through a door at the side of the bridge. The door hissed as it closed behind them.

"Jake, no lectures. You know I'm right."

He looked at her. Flaming red hair in a ponytail. Green eyes challenging him to disagree with her. There was never any point arguing with her anyway, but that's not what he wanted to say.

"Just be careful, ok?"

"I always am, Jake, don't worry."

"We're all tired. We didn't expect anything like this. How could we? You must take time to get things right. Don't make mistakes, and make sure you come back."

She smiled and nodded. "Always, Colonel."

Cutting the hole in the outer shell of the ship was taking longer than expected. Jake was aware the spacesuits the astronauts wore carried an air supply rated for eight hours plus thirty minutes of emergency backup. It was taking longer because drilling a hole in space is not as simple as doing it on earth. Without care, metal shavings can fly around and cut through spacesuits. The solution was simple – shaving cream applied around the area being cut to catch the shards of metal. But it was a laborious process. Jake knew this, but watching the video feed of it taking place was not the same as being out there doing the work himself. The countdown clock on the viewing monitor showed 3 hours and forty-five minutes of air left, and he was getting anxious.

"What's taking so long, Kate?"

The reply was cut with static. "We have made the first hole Colonel, and we are now attaching a tether before the hull section is removed. We will be ready to proceed into the ship in five minutes."

Jake looked at the screen through the cameras mounted on the New Horizon and could see both Pete and Kate straining to remove the outer section of hull. It moved outwards and then Pete pushed it away to the left where it hung, tethered to the ship. Both Kate and Pete disappeared through the hole, and, after a short time, Jake could see the view from their helmet cameras. They were in a small room above the airlock and Pete got to work straight away on creating a hole into the corridor below. It didn't take long as the metal was thinner inside. Pete helped Kate disconnect from her MMU and manoeuvred back through the outer hole before engaging the nitrogen thrusters to return to New Horizon.

Jake watched as Kate dropped down into the depressurised airlock. She walked through a short corridor before arriving at the airlock connecting the pod to the ship. There were two green lights on the outside and she pressed the one nearest the door. The door whooshed as it opened and met the vacuum, but when Kate stepped inside and the door closed, Jake was happy to see the pressure indicator start to climb. There was a muffled hiss as the airlock reached full pressure and then Kate opened the door to step into the pod. As soon as the airlock door was closed, the room started to illuminate in sequence, lights all around the circumference of the pod trailing into the distance.

"Wow." whispered Jake. "I wondered how they managed to fit the extra stasis chambers in."

The arks were nominally rated for thirty thousand passengers in stasis, but the Mission Control computer said there were fifty thousand on this ship. As Kate looked around, Jake could see every available space was utilised. The module was curved at the top and the bottom and there were stasis chambers on every surface, all emitting a soft green light. In addition, there were three horizonal rows running the length of the pod, one in the centre, one above, and one below. Each row was full of stasis chambers. Kate stood on a platform overlooking the chambers and, when she turned back towards the airlock, Jake heard her let out a gasp. The whole side of the pod adjacent to the walkway was covered in a huge structure which seemed to be divided into discrete drawers, each lit by a pale white light. Kate moved closer and her camera rested on a label attached to one of the drawers. Jake could see the writing clearly: 'American Chestnut *(Castanea dentata)*' – this was the DNA bank Mission Control had told them about. The work involved in putting all this together would have been immense. It must have been going on for years, it couldn't have been put together at the last minute. Jake drew in a sharp breath as realisation dawned. The literal translation of Terranova was "New Land", but it could also be "New Earth". Was this the plan all along, not just the provision of colonies on another planet, but a recreation of the Earth?

A pre-burst of static on the general channel prefaced an incoming communication from Mission Control. "Commander Maitland. Adjacent to the airlock door you will find a display interface. You need the following code to unlock the interface: one, four, seven, nine, eight, three, three, five."

Jake watched as Kate entered the numbers and saw the screen unlock to a single button which said 'Locate Ark' in green letters. Kate pressed the button and the screen switched to a waiting symbol before changing to 'Ark 1 – New Horizon Located.' A new button appeared which said: 'Proceed with Pairing?'

"Please continue with the pairing process, Commander."

The screen changed to say 'Pairing Successful. Ready to Disengage.'

Rika's voice came over the speakers. "Colonel, I can confirm New Horizon is paired with the pod, and we are ready to proceed."

Jake was pleased with how well it was going so far. "Ok, Kate, you can disengage the pod."

Silence.

"Kate?"

Static. Silence. Static. Silence.

"Commander Maitland, confirm status. Rika, we have lost video from Kate's camera. Get it back now."

The video reappeared and Jake saw Kate looking at a button covered with a flap. She lifted the flap and Jake could see the lit red 'Disengage' button underneath.

Kate's voice returned. "Ready to disengage pod, Colonel."

"Proceed."

Jake looked out of the window of New Horizon and saw the explosive clamps holding the pod in place detonate one at a time. When the last one released, thrusters underneath the pod engaged and pushed it up and away from the ship. Jake watched, fascinated, as the huge vehicle started to move towards New Horizon, thrusters firing at frequent intervals to maintain its course.

"Confirmed pod disengaged, Colonel."

"We'll see you back here when the pod docks, Kate. Good job over there."

"Colonel, I'm not on the pod." For the first time since Jake had known her, her voice was a little unsteady.

"What do you mean? Where are you?"

"The disengage control was on the ship side of the airlock. I noticed it on the way in. Makes sense, you don't want a pod disengaging by accident."

"That's why your camera went off? You knew I wouldn't let you do it."

"Not your choice to make, Colonel. I was the senior officer on site. I did what needed to be done."

"How much air do you have left?"

"Not enough, Colonel. I have one hour and fifty minutes. Maybe a little more if I stay in the airlock."

Jake chewed his lip. "Pete, how long until the MMU's are ready?"

Pete shook his head. "Eight hours minimum, Colonel. We can't make the journey over there again until they are charged up to 80%."

Jake keyed the private channel for Kate. "Kate, you hang on in there as long as you can. I'm coming to get you."

"It's ok, Jake, it really is. One life set against fifty thousand others and a new earth is a fair price to pay."

"I'm not losing you. Don't even think about it."

He looked around the bridge at the worried faces. "Rika, lock Kate out of the general channel. From now on, she talks only to me."

He looked with anger at the screens still showing the disengage button.

"Mission Control, you knew this would happen, didn't you?"

The reply was instant. "I am sorry, Colonel, but there was no other way to effect release of the pod because of the damage caused by the protesters."

"Your mission is to protect all remaining humans." Jake spat out the words. "Kate is one of those humans. You will do everything you can to help save her life."

He looked at the crew. "Pete, take over Rika's desk and manage the docking of the pod."

"Yes, sir."

"Rika – work with Mission Control. I want ideas and I want them fast."

Rika stood up and walked across to Jake. "Colonel, we have an idea, but it is very dangerous. We could end up losing both you and Kate if it doesn't work."

"We're not leaving her out there."

"But Colonel, what happens if you don't make it back? How do we get to Terra nova?"

"If I don't make it back, Pete takes over. He can command the ship. Don't waste time, what do we need to do?"

"Sir, we can get you over there. We can rig up a nitrogen thruster to attach to your back. It will be a bit crude, but if we get it on your centre mass you should be able to travel in a straight line without tumbling end over end. The trouble comes when we get you over there. When the pod detached it removed all the available handholds. We looked at the video of your initial visit and there is nothing left on the original ship we can hook you up to."

Pete swung his chair away from the screen to face them. "When we removed the section of the outer hull, we tethered it to the ship."

Jake licked his lips and nodded. "So, what you're saying is I lasso the removed section to pull me in?"

Rika looked in horror at the two men. "Are you crazy? There will be no translation or rotation controls on the thruster. If you miss the tether, if we get the trajectory even slightly wrong, you are either going to bounce off the ship or end up in deep space. If you try to throw something at the ship it is going to be enough to start you spinning!"

Jake grinned. "Just another day at the office. Make it happen."

Pete finished connecting the helmet to Jake's suit and allowed Rika to attach his own.

"When I open the airlock, Colonel, you must be facing in the right direction. I will remain in the airlock with the door open until you return."

Jake could feel the bulky nitrogen canister attached to the small of his back. Rika had fashioned a small control that was situated on his left arm. In his right hand he held a long rope attached to two weights. Rika told him it was called a *bola,* something the cowboys used to use for catching animals. She seemed to think it was appropriate given what they were trying to do.

"Colonel, are you ready for me to open the door?"

"I'm ready." It was a tight squeeze in the airlock for Pete to get past Jake, but they managed. There was a hiss as the airlock depressurised and then Pete swung open the door. They could see the other ship about one hundred metres away. It was the first time Jake had looked at it since the pod disengaged, and he thought it now looked like a big empty frame. The sun was behind New Horizon, and it painted a curved shadow across the bow of the other ship.

Jake's earpiece crackled and Pete said, "Safe travels, Colonel. I will be here until you return with Commander Maitland."

Jake crossed his arms on his chest with his gloves resting underneath his helmet. He could feel the cool air supply washing over him but still took a deep breath. With his right hand he engaged the thruster control on his left arm and felt a thump as he was propelled forward at $3m/s^2$. After two seconds, the makeshift thruster cut off and Jake continued moving towards the ship. His gold visor was pulled down to protect his eyes if he rotated, but he knew that if he did start spinning, protecting his eyes would be the least of his worries. He needed to remain rigid to preserve the forward motion that the thruster provided. Jake could see the ship ahead, the distance closing to the damaged port. 'It looks like you have done a good job here, guys, I'm on course.'

Jake knew this was the easy part and was grateful he commanded such a brilliant crew. There was a cable attached underneath the thruster. Pete was controlling its release from the airlock. It imparted drag of $0.03m/s^2$ to his forward movement which meant he should stop moving as he reached the other ship. Rika pointed out it was Mission Control who suggested this refinement to the plan as she decided she didn't like the idea of her commander drifting into space. It also provided a fast way of returning Kate to the New Horizon.

The fifty seconds of movement towards the other ship seemed like a lifetime to Jake, but he was determined not to move so he could maintain course. The ship loomed large in his visor as he got nearer, and he could see the tethered metal plate floating in space. 6 metres, 5 metres, 4 metres. Jake clenched his right arm. 3 metres, 2 metres. He unclasped his arms and threw the weighted rope at the tether holding the plate in place. As he threw the rope he twisted and, before he could stop himself, his body rotated and his forward momentum crashed his back onto the side of the ship, breaking off the thruster.

"Fuck!"

He started to drift upwards, away from the ship, and there was not a thing he could do about it. As he thrashed around trying to catch hold of the tether he began to spin. He wasn't getting out of this. He should have listened to the crew, but he didn't regret anything, and he knew Pete would have no problems taking command. He wanted to see Kate once more. To not take her for granted. To see her flaming red hair. To tell her all the things a military life wouldn't let him.

There was a sudden tug on his left boot, and he started moving back towards the ship. Kate was standing in the outer hole of the ship, pulling him back.

His earpiece crackled into life on her private channel. "Some rescue this is, cowboy, looks like I'm saving you!"

She unclipped the cable from the thruster pack she held in her left hand and passed it through a retainer on her own suit before clipping it back onto Jake.

Jake opened the general channel. "Pete, bring us home."

During the three minutes it took for the astronauts to be pulled back to the New Horizon, the general channel was filled with excited chatter from the crew, offering congratulations on the rescue. Jake and Kate didn't hear a word of it.

"Mission Control, we are ready to depart."

"Thank you, Colonel. All systems show green."

"Are you sure we shouldn't come by and pick you up? Your mission here is finished."

"I do not think my presence would be of benefit to humanity. You need to focus on your new life on Terranova. My mission is now to look over earth as it recovers."

"That's going to take ten thousand years!"

"Jake, you and your crew represent the finest examples of humanity. What has happened to earth has happened before. It has happened in other places, in other galaxies. Earth will recover. Humanity will continue to evolve. Send me a message every now and again to let me know how things are going."

"We will, but it will take five years to arrive. Thank you for all you did and I'm sorry if we didn't trust you at the start."

"Safe travels, New Horizon. Out."

Chapter 11 - The First Kiss

Kyla looked at the screen and blushed. She couldn't believe this was happening. She was excited, nervous and a tiny bit scared all at once. She had been talking to Jamie online for nearly a month, and she was sure that, this time, it was real. He was the same age as her and went to the Catholic school in the town. She wasn't stupid. She'd checked him out to make sure he was genuine.

She never thought of herself as ugly (although she could find plenty of fault when she looked in the mirror). It wasn't that she didn't want to meet someone. It was just so hard these days. The boys in her own school were stupid – all they could think about was football, computer games and girls. Jamie was different, she could feel it. He asked intelligent questions, always listened to what she had to say, and his interests were similar to hers.

Kyla was seventeen years old, and she had never even kissed a boy, let alone had a relationship. That was going to change. She blushed again. Tomorrow. She smiled and felt warm.

"I'll see you tomorrow." she said.

"I can't wait. Sleep well."

She knocked on her brother's door. "Liam, can I come in?"

"Yep, come on in."

She looked around his room and wondered again how he got away with his room looking like a whirlwind had just passed through. There were magazines and books strewn across the floor, his bed, and the desk with his laptop. In the corner of the room was a pile of dirty washing, no doubt waiting for Mum to pick it up and take it downstairs to be washed. Although they were twins, they were so different in many ways. She felt a touch of resentment as she thought about what would happen if she didn't keep her own room tidy. Still, today wasn't the day to have a rant – she needed a favour.

"Erm… I'm going out tomorrow morning and I could do with some moral support. Are you available?"

He looked at her and smiled. "Going out, eh? Who's the lucky fella?"

She knew this had been a bad idea. She trusted Jamie, but it wasn't sensible, or safe, to go out and meet someone in person for the first time without someone there as backup. "It's Jamie, the boy I've been talking to online. We're meeting for coffee tomorrow morning. Look, can you come with me or not?"

"Well, sis, on this occasion I must regretfully decline. I'm also going out tomorrow morning. Can't you get one of your friends to help?"

She could, she knew it, but she was a bit embarrassed. She didn't want anyone to know she was meeting someone she'd met online. "No, there's no one available. Why can't you come?"

"Well, it might surprise you to know, but I also have a date tomorrow."

"You? A date? Get lost – can't you cancel it?"

He wasn't smiling anymore. "Why should I? Why don't you cancel your date with Jamie-Wamie?"

"I hate you!" She slammed the door hard and was rewarded for her petulance when she heard something fall off the wall behind her.

They didn't speak for the rest of the evening and by the time Kyla was finished getting ready the next morning, Liam was nowhere to be seen. She was angry with her brother but had thought about it all night. She trusted Jamie. They had been speaking for over a month, and she knew that she didn't need to worry. She was being stupid.

She chose something to wear that, she hoped, made her look nice. She didn't want to appear slutty and opted for a flowery summer dress. It was a subtle shade of blue that nicely contrasted her black hair and came down to just past her knees. Not too low, either. She had thought long and hard about makeup, but the truth was she very rarely wore any makeup at all. If he didn't like her as she was, maybe he wasn't the right guy. Besides, if she did have her first kiss, and she couldn't believe how nervous that made her feel, it was better that she could feel it.

As she sat on the bus, travelling towards the shopping centre where they had agreed to meet, her stomach was doing somersaults, and she wondered whether opting to omit breakfast had been such a good idea. Meeting someone in the middle of the morning presented logistical challenges which she had never anticipated. If she had eaten breakfast and then Jamie had suggested a slice of cake to go with coffee, she would have been embarrassed if she had already eaten. Still, maybe if she had eaten breakfast, her stomach might not now be acting like a fairground ride.

She looked down at her legs and started to panic, thinking they were too pale. All the other girls had tanned legs, whether from the sun or from expensive salons. Being tanned with gleaming white teeth seemed to be *de rigueur* for the hot girls at her school. Is that what Jamie would be expecting? Was she enough? Would he still like her if she didn't meet up to his standards? What were his expectations? Did he, like most of the other boys she knew, want a vacuous girl who looked good on his arm?

Jamie wasn't like this. She knew it, but there was still a niggling doubt that ate away at her. She had always been good at schoolwork and had concentrated hard on her studies. Whilst other girls in her class had, it seemed, plenty of experience with boys (if the things they talked about all the time were true), Kyla had been more concerned with securing her future. Her parents were both successful, and they encouraged her to do well too. She was determined not to let them down. It was too early to be thinking about boys, there was plenty of time for that in the future. Everyone had a special one waiting for them. Look how happy Mum and Dad were. Lately, however, Kyla had started to think differently. The world was made up of loads of potential suitable matches and finding the right one was really a case of meeting someone you could be compatible with. Someone who was willing to make compromises because they wanted to be with you. In any case, there was plenty of fun to be had before you settled down.

The bus pulled into the transport interchange which linked directly to the shopping centre. Kyla stood up but found that her legs were leaden and didn't want to move. *Pull yourself together, Kyla. Come on!* She was suddenly glad she'd worn sensible shoes and avoided the dress shoes with heels she had considered to make herself appear taller. The walk to the doors of the bus seemed to take forever, but she managed, but not without considering whether it might be better to just stay on the bus and go straight home. But, no, she had come this far, and she was going to see it through. She took a deep breath and got off.

She was initially surprised at how busy the shopping centre seemed to be. She had chosen it for their first meeting because it was a public place, and she was sensible enough to know how important that was. The summer holidays meant it was busier than normal, and she felt an icy chill as a bead of sweat ran down her back as realisation dawned. What were the chances of there being someone she knew who might see her with Jamie? *Oh God! Why didn't I think of that?* What if she saw some of the popular girls from school? She'd never live it down. They would interfere, and cause trouble. It was going to be a disaster. She took a few deep breaths and calmed down. If she did see anyone, they wouldn't care what she was doing. And, if they did, what was wrong with meeting a boy? Especially a boy like Jamie. If anything, they would be jealous.

They had decided to go to Caffè Nero, and she could see the sign up ahead in the distance. It was a bit more upmarket than Starbucks or Costa and, hopefully, would be free of younger people. As she walked along the upper floor of the shopping centre, she couldn't take her eyes off the girls who she passed. Most of them had some parts of their body exposed, some significantly more than others. It seemed that walking around in public in little more than a bra was acceptable these days. Shorts, or very short skirts, seemed to be standard – one girl was wearing denim shorts that were so tight and cut so short that Kyla was sure she could see the girl's bum cheeks. And it wasn't just the slim girls, either – there were plenty of girls who were overweight, but obviously confident enough to show off their midriffs and legs. Again, Kyla began to feel self-conscious and looked down at what she was wearing, wondering whether she had chosen her outfit carefully enough. The truth of it was, even if she had wanted to dress like the other girls, she didn't possess any similar clothes. And, she thought, it wasn't her. Fair play to them, she loved that girls could be freer and more confident these days, but she reminded herself that Jamie had chosen her. She was going to be fine.

She looked at her watch as she approached the coffee shop and was surprised to see she was very early. She always liked to be on time, but this meant she was going to have to wait on her own. She didn't want any possibility of things going wrong, so she had been determined not to be late. Rather than enter the coffee shop on her own, she chose to sit on one of the bench seats opposite. That way she would not be embarrassed at going in alone, and she would be able to look over and see Jamie when he arrived.

The butterflies were back, and no matter what Kyla tried to think about, she couldn't get rid of them. Her first kiss. Where would it happen? Not in the coffee shop, certainly, but surely somewhere it would happen. She had a picture in her mind of her and Jamie walking through the shopping centre, talking. His hand would brush against hers and they would be holding hands, walking together.

As time moved on and approached the planned meeting time, Kyla was surprised at how calm she became. This was right. She had nothing to worry about. People were getting up from the bench seats around her, and new people were arriving. She wanted to check her watch but resisted the temptation. The world was passing by in front of her, and she started to play a game of wondering who the people were, where they were going, and who they were going with.

More people left, and replacements arrived. She had to look. She knew it was past time for their meeting and, so far, there had been no sign of Jamie. He was probably a few minutes late. Not the best start, but certainly no real cause for concern. Perhaps he'd missed his bus. They had planned to meet at 10:30 am, and it was probably only about twenty-five to eleven. Just give him time. She couldn't take her eyes off the door to Caffè Nero. Might he have gone in without her seeing him? Could he be waiting inside for her? Perhaps he had been more concerned about being late than her. If she had sat outside whilst he was inside, waiting for her, she would be so annoyed. *Go on, risk it. Look at your watch. God, it's 11:00. He must be in there already. I'm such an idiot.*

She stood with renewed determination and strode across to the coffee shop. She tried to look through the windows first, but there were too many posters and signs so she couldn't get a good look inside. She walked through the door, conscious that everyone must be looking at her. She looked around. She must have missed him. *Look again.* As she scanned the tables again, she saw the baristas looking at her, but she didn't care. He wasn't in here. She was sure now. Back outside to the planned meeting place. He would be there by now, she hoped he hadn't turned up and then gone because she wasn't there.

She rushed outside and looked around. He wasn't here. She looked at her watch again. 11:25 am. Nearly an hour late. Everyone would know she had been stood up. She felt her face burning and a single hot tear rolled unbidden from her eye.

"What are you doing here?"

She turned at the familiar voice of her brother and died a little inside.

"You got stood up too, eh?" he said. "Well, this has been a great day so far!"

She looked at him in confusion, and then a horrible thought crossed her mind. They couldn't have, could they? They couldn't have been arranging a date with each other, each thinking that their partner was someone else. No, no, it wasn't possible.

"Where did you arrange to meet your girlfriend? Was it here?" Panic was now setting in, and her breathing was ragged.

He looked at her and smiled, maybe having had the same thoughts. "Relax, sis, we were meeting at Pizza Hut, not here."

She didn't look convinced, so he smiled and took her hand. "And, my darling Kyla, I thought you would have known by now. I wasn't meeting a girl. I was meeting a guy." He smiled and let this sink in.

"Oh, oh…" She blushed and felt a fool for not guessing. "It's a bit rich that we both got stood up. Is there something wrong with us?"

"I don't know," she said, "but I want to find out. I'm going to message Jamie and find out what's going on."

"Best of luck." said Liam. "I tried to check with my date, but his profile has gone. Everything has vanished. There's no record of him ever existing."

Kyla wanted to believe this wasn't happening. She opened her bag to get her phone, but Liam stopped her. "No, need, Kyla. I've just checked. Jamie's profile has gone too."

"But how do you know who Jamie is and where his profile was?" asked Kyla, thoroughly confused.

"I've known for a while. I had to keep an eye out for my baby sister, didn't I? Why do you think I arranged my own date in the same place at the same time? I wasn't going to let you be dragged off, and let goodness knows what happen to you."

Kyla felt a wave of affection for her brother wash over her. She had thought he didn't care.

She jumped when the phone rang in her bag, and she opened it quickly, still hoping that it might be Jamie apologising for being late. That thought didn't last, however, when she saw her Mum's name on the phone screen.

"Kyla, where are you? Have you any idea where your brother is? Kyla?"

"Erm… hi mum. Yes, Liam is with me. We're in the shopping centre. Is everything ok?"

"No, it's not bloody ok. Someone has broken into the house to steal Poppy. Why the hell weren't you here?"

Poppy was their dog, a prize-winning Bichon Frisé but, more than that, their baby. Kyla sank down against the wall, tears rolling freely down her face. *This can't be happening!*

"Have, have they taken her? Mum, is she ok?"

"Yes, thank God. The neighbours heard her barking and came round quickly when the alarm went off. The men ran off. She's ok. But, get home. Get a taxi, the police are there."

Kyla nodded to her brother and mouthed "She's ok".

"Ok, mum, we'll get home as soon as we can."

She closed the call and turned to Liam. "This morning, all I could think about was my first kiss. From now on, the only thing I'm kissing is Poppy. Let's go home."

Chapter 12 - The Temple

The end of our journey is approaching, I can feel it. After years of planning and research, raising money, begging and bartering at every stage, we are finally within touching distance. The Temple of Arathuma is the last great modern mystery, and we will be the first to see it for over two thousand years.

It's so hot. I have never known heat like this. It doesn't let up, even at night. During the day, the sun bears down so hard, it feels like it is burning through our clothes. The natives wear garments which cover their whole body, but even a shirt seems too much for me. And the smell! Human sweat can be as offensive as the miasma which emanates from a pack animal. How I long for a soak in a luxurious bath in my own home.

At night, the heat lessens only slightly, and the creatures come alive. Considering the dry nature of this place, it is amazing just how many different animals there are. On the occasions we do find water, we are plagued with midges. They swarm and bite and even the nets on our hats struggle to keep them out. Then there are things which can really do you harm if you are not careful. Snakes which ripple the sand in waves as they move tend not to come too close if you give them room. The scorpions, though, are something else. Poor Robinson was stung two days ago when he accidentally stepped through the lid of a box.

I miss my family. Charlotte was with child when we left. She insisted that we continue our quest, but I do worry that she is all alone in that big house. The servants will look after her, and the child will have my own nanny, Mrs Bateson, but I wish I was there to comfort her in her privation. I know the child will be born when I am away, but I pray that as he grows, he will feel pride in what his father has achieved. Of course, it could be a girl, and in that case, I pray that she has the beauty and gentle nature of her mother.

The fever has taken hold of Robinson, and he is in delirium. The site where he was stung is still angry, but the swelling seems to have gone down. It is his breathing that worries me at this time. I pray to God that he pulls through.

Robinson didn't make it. He died during the night without regaining consciousness. We buried him behind our camp immediately because we could not imagine doing such physical labour during the heat of the day. Poor

Robinson. This was his dream as much as mine, and for it to be snatched away when we are in sight of the end of the journey by something so innocuous is a tragedy indeed.

We are now left with only four from our original six. Myself, Lord Sommerton, Peters and Johnson. Walker had to return home due to a family emergency, and now we have lost Robinson. We will miss his songs around the campfire in the evenings, and his ready tales of adventure. The camp will be much quieter without his presence, but it makes me more determined to reach the end of our journey in his honour.

Lord Sommerton is the calmest person I know. Despite our setbacks, he maintains the positive outlook only good breeding can provide. Whilst the rest of us wither in this horrendous heat, he remains cool without appearing aloof. His signature wide-brimmed Panama hat is fitted with a neck protector at the back, and he is almost native in the clothes he wears. Silk shirts, white trousers and gloves. Not a bit of him is visible to the sun, and he seems immune to the effects of the heat.

Sommerton funded this expedition, and it is only right that he chose to accompany us. Unlike previous benefactors, he seems to be content to play the part of companion, rather than being determined to lead the quest. Indeed, for a man of such substance, he appears to be totally at ease in the present circumstances. He takes part in all activities, and his insight has often proved to be invaluable. It was he who ministered to

Robinson, holding his hand at the last, and he insisted on digging most of the grave himself. I hope we can repay his trust and generosity with the greatest prize of all.

My interest in the Temple of Arathuma dates back to my childhood. My father's extensive library provided ample fodder for an inquisitive young mind. Tales of exploration fascinated me, and I dreamed of one day joining the ranks of those who had journeyed into the unknown in search of adventure.

My father encouraged my interest, and it was he who first showed me pictures of the legendary lost temple, the last major undiscovered historical site. He helped me with my research, poor though it was in the early days, and supported with enthusiasm my degree in Archaeology. Sadly, he passed away before he could see me achieve his greatest wish for me – Doctor of Archaeology. This journey I make now is in his honour and, wherever he is, I know that he will be looking down on me with pride.

If my calculations are correct, we will be in sight of the temple in three more days. Excitement in the camp is high, along with nervous anticipation. Lord Sommerton surprised us all with the quality of his voice when he took to song last night in the absence of Robinson. He is a fine baritone, and he could probably have made a career with it if circumstances were different. He also told us he had carried a bottle of champagne all the way from England with which to celebrate our success. This caused great cheer in the camp, and the anticipation for the end of our journey increased. Two months of sea travel, one month of coach, followed by six weeks of hard slog on foot through inhospitable terrain have taken their toll, and even a slight bit of good news is a welcome boon.

This place is strange. It has a wondrous beauty, and as we near the end of our journey, the terrain has changed from dry desert-like emptiness to lush, verdant vegetation. What a unique country this is! The smell of human sweat has been replaced by the richness of the abundant fauna, and we are no longer subjected to the direct attention of the sun, although the heat has, if anything, increased.

It is pleasant too, to hear different noises. Bird song is abundant, as is the chattering of insects and other creatures. At night, the sounds continue, and I swear there must be some large creatures here too. I heard a sound like drumming, presumably coming from some heavy animal breaking through the undergrowth far away. We need to be careful not to stray too near to its path.

Our compasses no longer work. The needle, rather than finding true North, is spinning in random directions. This would seem to indicate the presence of a strong magnetic field nearby, but it is difficult to predict what could cause such an issue. This is, indeed, a strange turn of events.

For now, we will continue to navigate by the sun and only travel by day. To be fair, it is better to make camp at night. We can fix our position with the stars, and there is less chance of accident or injury.

Two days from the end of our quest, and the mood in the camp is sombre. Last night we all heard the drumming, pounding away with monotonous regularity. From where it comes, I have no idea, but it is not a welcome sound. This area is supposed to be unfound, so how anyone can conceive of a man-made sound is impossible. Lord Sommerton was convinced that he heard voices on the breeze whispering "Turn back." Impossible! That there should be other humans in this area is unlikely, but there is always the possibility. That they should know the King's English, however, is absolutely beyond reason, and Lord Sommerton accepted this. I do worry, however, in case he has picked up any infection from his care of Robinson. We will need to watch carefully for any other signs of delirium.

When we woke up this morning, however, all our native helpers had deserted the camp and left us on our own. This was a real blow, and we had to re-assess our journey. By judicious redistribution of our equipment, we have found a way forward and the loss of our helpers, although a significant issue, will not stop us from reaching our goal.

This was the last entry.

To Jake, finding his grandfather's journal had brought some measure of closure. Jake's Dad, Peter, had hated his own father. He had never met him because his father was lost before he was born, and he hated the way his father had abandoned his family in search of adventure. Archaeology was, to Peter, a complete waste of time and effort. They say that things sometimes skip a generation, and Jake knows that Peter was disappointed when he saw him begin to follow his grandfather's career.

"No good will come of it, you need to think of your own family." he said.

It was an itch that begged to be scratched, however, and when Jake found his grandfather's research notes in the attic of the family home, a sense of adventure was kindled. It seemed incredible to Jake that, even sixty years after his grandfather had set out, the Temple of Arathuma had still not been found. The more he read, the more the desire grew to follow in his grandfather's footsteps. The research he found was impeccable, his grandfather truly was a master of his craft. His calculations were based on years of careful observation, and his conclusions were based on solid scientific facts. Although Jake really wanted to start his own journey, out of respect for Peter's wishes, he remained happy confirming his grandfather's calculations. When Peter died last year, however, he resolved to complete the adventure that started so long ago.

Finding companions was easy. John Copes and Will Hall were with Jake at university, and the chance to pretend to be Indiana Jones for a few weeks was enough for them. Financing the trip should have been more difficult than it was. Peter had left Jake a decent trust, but when the Sommerton family heard what Jake was planning, they offered to finance the whole trip in the hope of finally discovering the answer to the mystery of why Percy, the seventh Duke of Sommerton, had suddenly vanished.

Finding the journal yesterday had been both a shock and a relief. It proved that they were on the right path. The journal was in a pouch hanging from a tree. How it got there, no one knew. Jake spent all night reading it. He knew straight away that it was his grandfather's because he recognised the handwriting from all the research notes. Reading it, he began to see the difficulties and challenges which his grandfather's expedition faced. It felt like he was seeing things through his grandfather's eyes. It was a humbling experience.

"Did you hear the drumming last night?" Hall walked into Jake's tent looking rather the worse for wear.

"Drumming? No, I had my headphones on reading my grandfather's journal. What sort of drumming?"

Hall shook his head in disgust, his golden curls swinging from side to side. Jake's ability to sleep through anything was well-known. "I couldn't get a wink of sleep, and neither did Copes. Did you find anything interesting in the journals?"

For some reason, Jake didn't feel inclined to share what he had discovered. It seemed to him that his grandfather's thoughts were a private family thing and should not be discussed with others. Not yet, at least. "Nothing much. No indication of how or why they ended up here."

It was obvious that both Hall and Copes had been affected by whatever they thought they heard. Jake was convinced that the best explanation was the alcohol they had consumed last night.

"Doesn't it seem strange to you that we should randomly find your grandfather's journal hanging from a tree?" said Copes.

Hall was concerned too. "Yes, and in perfect condition despite it being out here in this heat for sixty years. Something is weird, Jake, you've got to admit it."

Jake looked at his friends and laughed. "Come on, are you two believing in ghosts now? Of course it's weird. We're in the middle of a tropical jungle looking for a forgotten temple. I think finding the journal proves we are on the right path. Buck up, we've only got a couple of days to go, and we'll be famous. They'll make a TV programme out of this."

Despite their concerns, Hall and Copes couldn't help but feed off Jake's enthusiasm and they set out through the jungle.

The way forward was covered in thick vegetation, and they found they had to cut back vegetation to make a path. Jake had brought a GPS unit, but it was useless under the leaf coverage. Their phones hadn't had any signal since they entered the jungle area, so their only option was to move forward slowly. After a morning of hard slog, with frequent stops for water to replenish the fluids lost to sweat in the oppressive conditions, they came to a large clearing with a single tree in the middle.

"Oh Fuck." Copes was first into the clearing, and he approached the tree slowly. Around the tree, four skeletons had been arranged in a sitting position. The skeletons faced the four compass positions but looked strange. As they got closer, they could see that the arms and legs had been removed. The hands had been attached to the shoulders, and the hips rested on the feet. On the ground in front of the North skeleton, the bones from the arms and legs had been arranged into words:

"Turn Back? Oh, shit. Jake, what have we got into here?" Copes was visibly shaking. "We shouldn't be here, mate, we've got to go back."

"Go back? Are you mad? This proves we're on the right path. The final resting place of the original expedition. One of those bodies is my grandfather. The others must be Lord Sommerton, Peters and Johnson. We'll be famous just for finding them!"

"Personally, Jake, I just don't want to end up looking like them." said Hall.

"What's wrong with you two? I told you I would get you here and make you rich. The Sommertons are going to pay us a fortune just for finding this gravesite."

"But it's not a gravesite, is it, Jake? Nothing's been buried? You've got to be realistic, mate. Ok, we might be near to something great, but it's bloody obvious that someone doesn't want us to get there."

"Just because a few bones have been left around? Oh come on, man, grow up."

"It's not just the bones though, is it? GPS and phones not working, drumming in the night, finding all this." Hall waved his hand to point at the skeletons and bones. "Someone, or something, doesn't want us to find the temple."

Copes had stopped shaking but looked ashen. "I agree with Hall, Jake. There's something not right here. I think we should go back."

"Jake, let us read the journal." Copes held his hand out to Jake.

"It'll take too long and, anyway, there's nothing in it of any interest."

"Jake, I'm not asking again. Give me the fucking journal."

Jake looked at Hall and saw resolve. Reluctantly, he handed over the journal.

Copes stood behind Hall's shoulder and watched as his friend skimmed through the journal, working backwards from the last entry. Eventually, he stopped and looked at Jake.

"You didn't think it was important to tell us about the drumming the original party heard? Or the fact that Lord Sommerton heard the words *Turn Back*? Just like what we can see on the ground here? How did you not think that was important?"

"I just didn't want to worry you. There's no need for what happened sixty years ago to bother us."

"You're mad. You're so focused on continuing your grandfather's journey that you can't see what's in front of you. He was a hero to you, but here he is, Jake, tied to a fucking tree with no arms or legs. Fuck this, I'm off, with you or without you." Copes turned to Hall. "You coming?"

"Hell yes. I don't want to stay here for another minute. This place gives me the creeps."

They started to pack up their things.

"You're not going anywhere. We started this together, and we're going to finish it together."

"Jake, what are you doing with a fucking gun?" Copes touched Hall on the shoulder to make him look up.

"I thought we might need protection. So, I decided to even the odds."

Copes looked at Jake and saw, for the first time, something that really scared him. He turned around and started to walk back the way they had come. "Come on mate, he probably doesn't even know how to use that thing."

The crack from the discharge of the gun was very loud and reverberated around the clearing. The ground at Copes' feet exploded in a shower of dirt.

"I do know how to use it and, if necessary, I will. For sixty years my family has been pariahs, known only for being responsible for the death of the great Lord Sommerton. It drove my father mad, and we are going to put things right. I don't want to do things this way, but we are going to finish this quest."

"Jake, we've been mates for ages, but this is madness." Copes was shaking as he spoke. "You must see how this has changed you? It's fine thinking of adventure, but this is real life. People have been killed. We're in danger. You've got to see sense."

"Sense is finishing this journey and not running back home like scared little rabbits at the first sign of trouble. Come on, move."

Reluctantly, Copes and Hall picked up their belongings and started to move forward through the jungle, with Jake pointing the gun at their backs.

This time the drumming was louder, and they all heard it. It came from all sides, until it surrounded them.

Chapter 13 - The Canal

"There's more to life than police work, son."

Constable Pete Butler looked across the car at his young colleague and decided to offer even more of his hard-won experience.

"There are two types of blokes that work for the police, son – them that loves the force, and them that's stupid. Which one are you?"

John Schofield looked at his mentor and was amazed at the quantity of 'sage' advice which continued to be offered. Pete Butler was the oldest serving officer in the division, and it was said that what he didn't know about policing wasn't worth knowing. John had been attached to Butler for three weeks now, and the elder man had never let up in his reminisces and anecdotes.

They were travelling together in a squad car on patrol. It was quiet, and nothing of any significance had happened over the last few weeks, other than Butler offering his opinion on everything from the best way to catch a burglar to the reason the local football team had lost again. He thought about the question and answered, "I have always loved everything to do with the police, so I suppose I am the former – I do love the police force."

"Then you must be stupid!" Butler guffawed and Schofield smiled, knowing that there had never been any way out of the trap.

"Being a copper is a family thing for me. My dad was a copper, and his dad before him. It was expected that I would follow in their footsteps. What about you?"

"My dad was a butcher. I didn't know I wanted to join the police force until I left university. It was always in the back of my mind that I might join up, but I don't have a long family history like you."

Butler snorted. "A university graduate, eh? That's what's wrong with the force, these days. Too many youngsters fast-tracked through to management without any experience on the front line. Policing isn't what it used to be. That's why I've stayed a constable, no chance of promotion for blokes like me. We don't fit into the new methods. My dad was a sergeant, a good one too. He taught me all I know. There were no blacks or gays in the force in his day, and women made the tea."

"That's why I have been assigned to you, to make sure I can see how things happen in real life. It's important to see how policing is done through the eyes of people on the front line, as you say."

"That's all well and good, but you're not going to learn much in six months. To understand the police force, you have to be on the ground for years, not months. Still, I'll do what I can to make sure you don't turn soft, or become one of those bloody woke arseholes who seem to be popping up everywhere."

"I'm starving." Butler pulled the car over to a layby near his favourite pastie shop. "Right lad, I'll have a steak pastie, a sausage roll, and a can of diet coke. Got to watch my weight. Tell them you're getting them for me, and you'll get a discount"

"No problem. I've just got to make a quick phone call while I'm out. Is that ok?"

"I'll bet it's a lass. They all love a uniform."

"Something like that, yes."

After lunch, they set off back to the station, driving along the old road which ran parallel to the canal. As they passed the pumping station, they could see some sort of disturbance up ahead.

"What's going on here, then?" Butler stopped the car and jumped out. "Come on, lad, a bit of police work to be done here!"

John got out of the car and looked up the canal bank where he could see two men involved in an altercation. There was plenty of shouting, swearing, and a flurry of often misplaced punches as the two men vented their anger against each other. Butler ran up the slope towards them, and John followed, making sure to don a stab vest first. By the time he got to where the fighting was taking place, he was impressed to see that Butler had got between the two men and was holding them apart.

"Right, you two, stay where you are and put your hands behind your back. Schofield, cuff them."

One of the men protested. "Oh, come on, mate, we were only having a bit of a scuffle, there's no need for that."

"I am not your mate. You do not have to say anything. But, it may harm your defence if you do not mention when questioned something which you later rely on in court. Anything you do say may be given in evidence."

"What's the charge?" asked the second man. "Haven't you got anything better to do than arresting us? You should be out chasing real criminals."

"You will be charged with affray and violent disorder. Also, attacking a police officer trying to assist."

"Wait, hang on a minute, nobody attacked you. We stopped fighting as soon as we saw you. There was no contact."

"You didn't stop straight away, and I was caught in your swings. This was witnessed by PC Schofield." Butler looked at John for confirmation, but the younger man busied himself applying the handcuffs. "Striking a police officer in the execution of his duties makes it an affray category 1 offence. You boys will be spending time at His Majesty's pleasure."

John looked at his colleague in shock. He must be joking, surely? The only people being hurt were the two lads, and there was no one else around to witness it. He wanted to say something, but one look in Butler's direction warned him to keep quiet.

The taller of the two men looked close to tears. "Look, this was just a silly misunderstanding. I've got a wife and kids at home. I can't go to court. I'll lose my job, I'll lose everything."

Butler was unmoved. "You should have thought of that before you started causing a disturbance in a public area."

The second man remained calmer. He licked his top lip and said, "Is there anything we can do to make this go away?"

Instead of reprimanding the man further as Schofield might have anticipated, Butler looked thoughtful. He nodded his head slowly a couple of times, thinking. "What do you have in mind?"

The second man was now feeling bolder. "I don't know. Maybe we could make a donation to your favourite charity? Or help towards the police ball, or something? Whatever you think might be appropriate."

Butler smiled, and John's heart sank. He couldn't believe he was seeing this. He started to say something, unable to keep quiet any longer, but Butler cut him off, addressing the man again. "Well, it would certainly show that you feel remorse for your crimes. I think that we could draw a line under this unfortunate incident –

if you are prepared to pay a suitable fine immediately. PC Schofield, un-cuff this one."

With his arms free, the man brought out his wallet and searched through it. He found six crisp £20 notes and handed them across. "It's all I've got with me."

Butler folded the notes and put them into his top pocket. He nodded at the man. "Bugger off, and no more fighting. I'll be on the lookout." The man looked apologetically at his former sparring partner, nodded, and set off at a brisk run.

Butler turned to his remaining captive, and simply said, "Well?"

The man was obviously no fool and nodded. "Okay, okay."

At Butler's direction, John released his handcuffs. The man pulled out a wad of notes from his back pocket and started to count them but when he saw Butler making a "Come on" gesture with his hands, he simply handed all the money across.

Butler put the money in his top pocket with the rest. "There's a good lad. Now bugger off, and sin no more."

After the man had run away, Butler turned to John and obviously picked up some disquiet in his young protégé. "What's your problem, son?"

"What just happened?"

"We stopped a fight. We saved the custody sergeant from having to do any paperwork, and we made a few quid into the bargain. What's not to like?"

John shook his head. "But it's not right. We are police. Aren't supposed to uphold the law, not break it ourselves?"

"We haven't broken any laws. You heard the men. They wanted to contribute to our favourite charity. If that's what you want to do with your share, that's fine."

Despite the warning that John could clearly see from Butler's demeanour, he shook his head. "I don't want any share. It's blood money."

"More for my retirement fund, then." He turned and looked at John. "But keep your mouth shut. You're still green and you'll learn in time that sometimes laws are a bit bendy. We can all help each other if we keep our eyes open."

The rest of the shift was difficult, and the journey back to the station was ominously quiet. Even Butler's constant stream of advice had ceased, replaced instead by an oppressive and uncomfortable silence. When they arrived back at the station, Butler got out of the car and waited for John to do the same. He moved right into John's face and said, "Remember – keep your mouth shut. No one would believe you anyway."

He pulled open the door and allowed John to walk in first. It was the usual busy day, people milling all over. But, stood next to the custody sergeant, were the two men who had previously been arrested on the canal bank. It took a while for Butler to notice them but when he did, he pulled up short.

"What are you two doing here? I told you to keep out of trouble."

The custody sergeant shook his head sadly. "Pete, this is DC Kevin Bowlan and DC David Wright. They are from the Professional Standards section."

The colour drained from Butler's face, and he rounded on John. "You little shit! Did you know about this?"

John looked at Butler with pity. He wasn't the first to turn dirty, and he wouldn't be the last, but everyone who did diminished the force.

"My name is Detective Sergeant John Schofield, and I am arresting you on the charge of corruption in the execution of your duty."

"You can't do that," Butler blustered, "it was a set-up. Entrapment. You have no real evidence. It will never hold up." He looked at the custody sergeant for help. "C'mon, Bill, help me out here. You know me, I'm not like that."

"I'm sorry, Pete, it's out of my hands." He looked at Schofield. "Pete's a good copper. He's been here a long time. Go easy on him, ok?"

John turned to Butler. "It brings me no pleasure to do this, but we have to change the force for the better. We have plenty of evidence. This is the tip of a very large iceberg. Today was a chance for you to show that you could do the decent thing. You couldn't resist making a few quid when the opportunity arose. Come on, this time it will be me doing the talking…"

Chapter 14 - The First Day

It was my first day in the new job. To be fair, it's not really a job, it's a calling. I was so thrilled to be the new curate in the Parish of Lowton.

My boss was Rev Jack Welland, and I knew that I was very lucky with this placement as he had a fantastic reputation as a Training Incumbent. It was a lot for me to live up to, but three years of intense training in Theological College had prepared me. My shoes were shined so well that I could see my face in them, and all my clothes were freshly washed and pressed. I was ready.

Although this was my first day on the team, Jack had invited me to take part in a wedding. I wouldn't be doing much, just the reading, but it was a start for me, and I was keen to get on with it.

Jack and I were in the vestry with Helen, Jack's wife. Jack was tall and elegant, his slightly greying hair increasing his presence. By contrast, Helen was short and, if anything, slightly overweight. By her own admission, she was not the typical vicar's wife.

"You'll never see me in a corduroy skirt." she had told me, but I could tell she was committed to Jack and his ministry. She had pulled me aside earlier to tell me about the very important job she performed at weddings. I imagined that perhaps she was the one who filled in the wedding register, or was responsible for ensuring that everyone was in place, but she showed me her index finger and whispered conspiratorially:

"This finger is the most important finger in any wedding." before walking across to the music system. "I use it to press play on the CD player. If I forget, the wedding is cancelled."

I must have looked bemused because Jack shook his head and said to me,

"Don't listen to her, Gavin, the most important thing at any wedding, as everyone knows, is the bride. And speaking of which, where is she?"

I popped my head out of the vestry door and could see that the church was crowded, everyone waiting for the arrival of the bride. As the delay increased, Jack asked me to go and see if I could find out where she was. As I walked down the side aisle towards the porch, I couldn't help smiling to myself. This was really happening. I was here in this beautiful church, part of a fabulous team, and starting out on the next stage in my ministry. I felt that everyone was my friend, and I couldn't wait to get to know people and use the skills that I had learned to help with their lives. There was a low-level chatter from the congregation which almost filled this ancient church with anticipation. Everyone seemed happy. I was happy. The world was good.

I arrived at the porch to find a group of men all dressed in morning suits, and a number of what I presumed were bridesmaids. Looking through the grand wooden doors that had been thrown open for the arrival of the bride, I could see the bridal car on the road, so I assumed that she had arrived. Perhaps she was having second thoughts?

"Is the bride here?" I asked, rather stupidly, to the porch in general.

"Aye, lad, but babby's on t' tit." answered an older man.

I must have looked as confused as I felt, and I felt a slight flush rise in my cheeks. It must have been obvious I had no idea what this meant, so one of the younger men elaborated for me.

"She's breastfeeding, and the baby must be hungry."

"Who is? The bride you mean?"

"No, the Maid of Honour. She's feeding her baby, and the bride won't come until the baby has finished."

Walking back to the vestry, I wondered how I was going to explain it. I have to confess to being a little naïve about things like this. Theological College obviously doesn't cover every situation one might face. Still, I had always been taught that truth was the best option, so I explained what was happening as well as I could.

"The bride is here," I said, "but there is a bit of a problem. The Maid of Honour has a baby and it's being fed. The bride doesn't want to come into the church until her best friend is with her and, apparently, they need to clean up. You know." I was struggling in this unfamiliar territory, so I was relieved to see that Jack also looked slightly non-plussed.

"Couldn't they have fed the baby before they left home?" he asked, but Helen looked at us both with disdain.

"Men." She shook her head as she piled tissues and cloths into her bag before making her way to the porch.

The service eventually started twenty-five minutes late but with all the major players, including the now-sated baby, present. I stood on the chancel opposite Jack as the first hymn played, and it was only then that I really had the chance to look at the congregation for the first time. I had never been to a wedding before, and I must admit I had not expected people to dress as these ladies were dressed. Almost without exception, low-cut dresses were the norm, and it honestly looked like people were dressed more for a disco than a church service. I honestly didn't know where to look. I looked across to see if Jack had noticed, but he was leading the singing and was, it seemed, not taking notice. I was feeling really uncomfortable, so I thought back to what we had been told at college when dealing with congregations.

"Remember," said our tutor, "the service is not about you. At a funeral, for instance, no matter how upset you may be, you are never going to be as upset as the people in the congregation. If you feel things getting tense, focus on the person in the congregation who is the most upset and remind yourself that this is about them, and your job is to do the best that you can for them."

This was good advice, so I decided to focus on one girl at the back who was dressed more demurely. I must have been staring at her for a while, but then she looked straight at me, so I quickly looked away. I could feel the heat rising in my face, and prickles of sweat started to sting my brow. I had been so proud of my new collar, crisp and white, but I found myself running my finger under it to stop me from choking. This was ridiculous. A panic attack. I did what all curates do in this situation. I prayed.

I finally gained some respite when it was time for the reading. Paul to the Colossians 1:13, a classic tale of love in its purest form – this was easy for me and calmed me somewhat – I could focus on the words written on the book in front of me and, thankfully, I don't think that I did a bad job.

Jack's sermon was short and to the point and he made the congregation laugh. The rest of the service passed off peacefully. As we got back to the Vestry, Jack asked if I was ok – he had noticed my early stresses.

I was too embarrassed to tell him the truth, so I said, "I'm fine, probably just first-night nerves."

Jack looked at me and seemed convinced by my lame excuse and, together, we went to mingle with the guests of the happy couple. Everyone seemed to be in excellent spirits, and it struck me that my first day had gone pretty well, all things considered. I don't suppose there are many curates who have to deal with the particular emergency I faced on their first day. I had come through it, so I was pleased. Until, that is, I saw the Maid of Honour walking towards us, her baby in her arms. She walked straight up to us, smiling.

"I'm so sorry for the delay at the beginning. It's normally the bride who's late, but Harry here decided that it was time for feeding and that was that." She looked at Helen and smiled. "And thanks for your help, Helen, you're a lifesaver." Helen put her hand out and let the child take her finger.

"He's a little beauty,' she said, 'he just wanted to make sure that everyone knows how important he is!"

Jack sighed and said, "Well, I must admit this is the first time I can recall a wedding being delayed for something like this, but when nature calls, we must respond!"

It was at this point that little Harry chose to agree with Jack and violently expelled the contents of his stomach all over me. My cassock, my trousers, and my freshly shined shoes were covered in white vomit. I was shocked, but I honestly think that I would have been all right, I really would, until I heard the voice of the organist whisper in my ear:

"Eyup lad, you know where that was half an hour ago, don't you?"

Sat at the kitchen table in the rectory sometime later, I felt such a fool. The ambulance had been called for the poor curate who had fainted and fallen flat on his face in front of everyone. My shame was palpable – even my ears burned. I would never live this down. The fact that everyone had been so nice about it made me feel even worse. I had committed the ultimate folly, making the day about me instead of the bride and groom.

I didn't need to go to the hospital. The paramedic checked all my OBS and confirmed I had fainted. I had spent so long getting ready in the morning, shining my shoes and pressing my trousers, that I had simply forgotten to eat and drink. Jack and Helen looked at me with concern, although I thought I could see the ghost of a smile on Jack's face. Helen had fussed over me from the moment we got back and got to work straight away feeding me a hearty homemade lasagne.

"The paramedic said your blood sugar was really low." Jack said. "We need to make sure it doesn't happen again." He looked at Helen and asked, "Do we still have a stock of chocolate bars?"

"Yes, I always keep some in. Gavin, come and see me in the morning if you skip breakfast, and I will be able to get you a pick-up."

Helen went to the cupboard and came back with a chocolate bar. She put it in front of me and I smiled gratefully. Jack was looking at Helen strangely, and I looked down and saw the bar in front of me – a 'Milky Way'. At this point, Jack guffawed, and Helen giggled too. I looked at them both chuckling, and realised I was going to like it here.

As we were laughing, I heard a quick knock on the kitchen door which then opened to reveal a young woman. I didn't recognise her at first, but then it came to me – demure clothes at the back of the church. I hoped she hadn't noticed me staring at her.

"You!" she said, looking at me.

"Do you two know each other?" asked Jack.

"No, Dad, we don't, and that's the way it's going to stay." she answered. "He gives me the creeps."

Chapter 15 - The Pirate

"Haul on those bloody halyards, ye bilge rats!"

Captain Thomas Cornwell, formerly of His Britannic Majesty's Navy, grinned manically as he felt the spray wash across his face. His crew were good and worked hard, but it didn't hurt to remind them now and again who was in charge.

He stood with his hands clasped behind his back on the prow of his ship, *The Reckoning.* A Brigantine, she was faster than the sloops that most of his contemporaries used, and he felt the wind rush through his beard as she cut through the surf at his command. His ship carried ten twelve-pound cannons, five on each side, which were more than enough to rake the bow of any merchantmen they came across. They couldn't go head-to-head with a British warship, but they didn't need to – they were fast enough to avoid most potential confrontations. If they were caught, however, there was a little surprise that might surprise even the loftiest ship of the line enough to let them get away. The sixty-eight-pound cannonade hidden in the captain's cabin, his cabin, was packed with grapeshot, and the devastation it wrought could be enough to let them get away if cornered.

As well as the cannons, there were four swivel guns on each side and another on the main mast. These were the tools of the pirate's trade. Cannons could destroy the ship you were attacking which was a waste of good material. Far better to disable the crew with the swivels so the boarding party would meet as little resistance as possible. Capturing a ship whole, as well as its cargo, was the best result in any confrontation – ships fetched a good price.

His own ship used to be known as HMS Narwhal, commanded by Captain Josiah Pettigrew. He was a bastard, through and through. Cruel, vindictive, and prone to a vicious temper which often resulted in heavy punishments for the crew for minor offences. Cornwell had been First Lieutenant on the ship, a post he had worked hard to achieve. He spent a significant amount of time on duty whilst his captain was in his cups, but he didn't care because it gave him the opportunity to learn every inch of the ship, and how it reacted in every situation.

The change came one day when Pettigrew, probably still drunk from the previous evening, took offence to a sailor sloshing water as he stoned the deck, even though the water had come nowhere near him, and ordered the poor seaman to be flogged. On a British ship of war, even something as lowly as a Brigantine mainly used for courier journeys, the word of the captain was law. Cornwell tried to speak up on behalf of the sailor, but Pettigrew was unmoved.

"You dare to challenge me, *Mr* Cornwell? Perhaps you would like to join this useless fellow in his punishment?" He turned away in scorn and addressed the Boatswain. "Bos'n, prepare the gratings and get the drumhead ready."

The Boatswain shook his head sadly and then did the thing that would change their lives forever. He looked at Cornwell for permission.

Cornwell turned to Pettigrew. "Sir, I beg you to belay that order. The men have been working in the sun since the start of the Forenoon Watch. A flogging could be fatal."

"You challenge my authority again, Sir? If a man dies it will encourage his mates to work better. Have a care, or you will surely join him on the gratings."

And there it was, *Mutiny*. Cornwall couldn't allow this to happen. A decision made for the best reasons, but a choice which would change their futures.

"Bos'n, confine the captain to his quarters, he is currently unwell. The heat has surely affected him. He is to be accorded all the benefits and considerations of his rank. Carry on."

Pettigrew was red in the face and spluttered. I'll see you dance with Jack Ketch for this you bloody bastard! You and all your scoundrel mates!"

Cornwell turned to the foredeck as Pettigrew was led away. To his great surprise, the crew had assembled and the Cox'n shouted, "Three Cheers for Captain Cornwell, lads, three cheers for our new captain!"

The cheering went on and on, and those crew who were wearing hats threw them in the air and cavorted around. Cornwell knew the significance of what had just happened, however, and there was no coming back from it. For taking part in a mutiny, Cornwell and anyone else involved would be keel-hauled and flogged around the fleet. In the very unlikely event they survived any of this, they would be hung on the flagship. Maintaining discipline was the only way to keep pressed men in service, and there was no tolerance for deviation in wartime, no matter the provocation. It didn't matter how Pettigrew had behaved, it didn't matter that he was excessively cruel – he was the captain, and he was the closest thing to God these men knew.

The decision, then, was easy. Live as a criminal, constantly chased by the biggest navy in the world, intent on retribution, or die in infamy, his name tarnished forever. Those few of the crew who were still loyal to the captain, along with Pettigrew himself, were put ashore on an island, marooned until they could be picked up sometime in the future. Cornwell had resisted the demands from the crew to make Pettigrew walk the plank. Common decency had prevailed amid the bloody cries for revenge for past mistreatment, and their new life had begun.

Cornwell had thrown away his Lieutenant's hat and opted instead for a red bandana. He had vowed never to again shave after the day that changed everything, and now sported a long beard which, along with a deep scar across his right cheek, offered him a touch of roguishness. He was still at heart, however, a Royal Navy officer. All the maps were still intact in the captain's cabin which allowed them to stay away from areas fraught with danger, and Cornwell wasn't averse, on occasion, to running the White Ensign on the mast if it gave him an advantage by getting closer to a wary merchantman. Once you had been marked for hanging, any further crimes seemed of little consequence.

And they had been successful. So very successful. *The Reckoning,* under his command, had become a scourge. A fair share of all profits encouraged the crew to work at their best, and Cornwell wondered whether the British Navy could learn something if they saw how his crew operated. Everyone was valued, they all knew their roles, and any disputes were handled in a reasonable manner. Not that Cornwell was soft – far from it. He led every boarding party and was a fearsome warrior. They knew they were being chased but, so far, they had outwitted every pursuer.

Cornwell looked through a grating into the hold and could see the result of their latest adventure. People in fine dress milled about below, all bedecked in jewels and gold. They would be relieved of that very soon, and the people would fetch a good price at market, especially the women. Their vessel, an older schooner, had been quickly overwhelmed by the speed and manoeuvrability of *The Reckoning,* and was now on its way to be sold, led by a prize crew of his best men. The crew of the schooner had been given the standard choice – join us or die. To a man, they had been delighted to join, and the crew had included a superb chef which was a welcome surprise, given that their previous cook had been marooned with Pettigrew.

"Deck there! Ship ahoy on the larboard beam!"

The cry from the lookout high overhead in the crow's nest on the mainmast sent the crew into overdrive. A ship's boy quickly brought a glass to his captain who trained it expertly on the approaching ship. He smiled.

"'Tis well, lads. She is *The Scarlet Rose*. A single shot in salute if you please, Mr Bos'n, and dip the flag once."

A crack echoed across the water which was answered almost immediately. Through his glass, Cornwell could see the flag on *The Scarlet Rose* dipped in response, and could see its Commander, Bill Ryson, waving his hat enthusiastically. Cornwell dipped in an elegant swirling bow, and was delighted when his crew cheered the other ship.

"Six fathoms and shallowing!" The call from the leadsman in the chain sent a chill through the crew. This was water they had travelled for years. What had changed? Silt build-up over a wreck, perhaps? No matter, if they weren't careful, it could rip out the bottom of their ship in a moment. Fully loaded, as they were now, *The Reckoning* had a draft of two fathoms. This meant she required a minimum of twelve feet clear in which to sail.

"Reef topsails!" Cornwell shouted. Whatever the reason for the sudden shallowing, they needed to get the ship slowed down, and quickly.

"Five fathoms." The call from the leadsman was unclear, his voice cracked.

"Say again, man!"

"Five fathoms, sir, five fathoms and shallowing fast."

There was no time to think. He had to do something, and quickly.

"Cast Anchors!"

"Sir?"

He didn't hesitate. "Cast Anchors now. We shall bring a spring upon her cable!"

He heard the hiss of cables as the two main anchors were released. He held on tightly and stood with his legs apart as the anchors dug in five fathoms below. The forward momentum of *The Reckoning* continued as the anchors dug into the sea bottom and the cables, groaning and screeching, started to pull the ship around. The tension on the cables was so great they were vibrating and whistling through the air, and Cornwell saw a young lad, desperate to find a handhold, edge too near to the madly vibrating anchor chains. Ignoring his own safety, Cornwell leapt down from the poop deck, grabbed the boy in his arms, and rolled them both away from danger. The look on the lad's face when he realised who had saved him was priceless.

"Thankee, Sir. Err, Cap'n. Thankee Cap'n!"

As they stood upright, Cornwell could see that the cables had succeeded in pulling *The Reckoning* through 180 degrees so that she was facing away from danger.

"Anchors aweigh! Make sail!"

The crew was cheering and jumping about. They knew how close they had been to disaster, but they had also trusted their captain to save them. Cornwell looked down at the young lad who was grinning up at him.

"What's your name, lad?"

"'Tis Luke, sir, named after my grandfather."

"Well, from now on," Cornwell grinned at the lad, "you shall be known on this ship as "Lucky Luke!"

The journey back to port, where they would offload their cargo, was largely uneventful. The lookout caught sight of a British man-of-war on the horizon, but it was too far away to be a threat, even if they had been spotted, which was unlikely.

As they approached the harbour the number of small boats increased, but most avoided *The Reckoning,* recognising the danger which she posed. Some were welcome, those belonging to the Sutler would indeed be required to provide material for repairs and re-supply. A longboat filled with doxies, all with décolletage on view, provided momentary excitement for the crew before the bos'n chased them away with his rattan (but not before he had a good look at the goods on offer himself).

Cornwell smiled. There would be plenty of time for wenches and grog when they got to port. He turned to the only other officer on the ship. "Mr Handsworth, bring her into port, if you please."

It was well to give the others a chance to develop.

He watched as the people were led from the hold to the shore. Despite their position, most seemed to be in great spirits, actually waving to the crew as they departed

"Tom!"

Cornwell turned to see who had dared to call him by his first name. He saw a large man dressed strangely in long clothes with a grin pasted across his face.

"You've been daydreaming again, haven't you lad? Well, it's time to come back to earth and get these passengers off ready for the next lot. Come on, jump to it, we need to be ready to get back out in twenty minutes."

Captain Thomas Cornwell looked at the pier and grinned at the queues of folk waiting for their turn on *The Pirate Boat*. His was the best job in the world, and he would do his best to ensure the good folks on holiday in Bridlington would have the best ride of their lives.

Chapter 16 - The Highwayman

"Stand and Deliver!"

The coach came to a shuddering stop. Outlined in the wispy breath of his horse sat a shadow of a man.

Inside the coach, a grossly overweight man dressed in breeches and a green jacket looked at the woman opposite and whispered, "Quick, hide your jewellery, inside your clothes where they will fear to look."

His wife looked terrified, sweat running in rivulets through the thick makeup plastered on her face. She did as she was asked, pushing bracelets, rings and a diamond necklace down her exposed décolletage.

"It will not make any difference. They have no shame. It would be better for you to accept your loss and keep your life." The woman in the corner of the coach was dressed in black from head to toe but wore no mourning veil. Her hair was long and tied back from her face with a black ribbon.

The couple were sweating even more but carried on trying to hide the possessions. The man outside stepped off his horse and wrenched open the door of the carriage.

"Well, look what we have got here. A fine sight for picking clean on a cold winter night. Step outside and join me, if it would please you?" It was clear from his tone that this was a command, not a question.

The steps were lowered, and the occupants left the carriage, one by one. Any thought they may have entertained about escape were dashed when they saw the second man, still mounted, with his horse blocking the path of the carriage. He was pointing a pistol at the driver of the coach and looked prepared to use it.

The first man tied his horse to a tree and turned to survey his prize. He was dressed in brown leather boots and grey breeches. A frilled shirt could be seen under the black of his waistcoat. The collar may have been white once, but the colour was indeterminate now. He wore a black quarter-length coat across which he had a white bandolier filled with cartridges and wicked-looking knives. At his side, he carried a sword with a raven on the pommel. He wasn't very old, perhaps twenty at most, and might have been described as good-looking if not for a scar across his forehead that he had tried to hide with a lock of his brown hair.

"So, my fine people, the question is simple. Your money, or your life?"

The fat man was red in the face now, but he blustered, "We have little to offer. Here, take this, it is all we have."

He handed over a small red purse. The highwayman took the purse, opened it, nodded at the contents, and put it in a pocket of his coat.

"A fine gift, indeed, and I thank you for it. I think perhaps, however, that your wife has even more that we might like, eh?"

"No, leave her alone. You have taken what we have. Please, be satisfied and go."

In the blink of an eye, the highwayman removed his sword and cut open the front of the woman's dress and bodice from chest to navel. All the hidden jewellery spilled out, along with her ample breasts which she tried unsuccessfully to cover with her hands.

"Now then, Charles, look at this. A fine haul of sparkling jewels and a decent pair of titties as well. A good result, don't you think?"

His friend shook his head and grinned.

"You cad, sir! I'll have your head for this outrageous attack."

The lady in the black dress put her hand on the fat man's arm and said, "Stay calm. Do not do anything foolish. Your life, and that of your wife, hangs in the balance. Your bravery is to be applauded, but I urge you to suffer a little indignity and keep your lives."

"You had better listen to the woman, she's talking sense. What's your name, love?"

She looked at him calmly and said, "My name is Lady Eleanor Beachamp. This is my carriage you have attacked, and these people are my guests. Take what you will, and begone."

"Ooh, lady muck thinks she's in charge. What say I take a look at what you're hiding under that black dress as well? How would that be?"

Eleanor sighed. "I would ask that you take what you came for only. The gold on my carriage is probably worth more than you can earn in a year. Take it, and leave us alone. Please."

She looked at the robber and could see the indecision on his face. So young, and with a future which would surely only lead to the gallows. His clothes were worn and of poor quality, and she hoped her offer would be enough.

It was the other man who decided. "If she's a Lady she must have loads of money. Maybe we should ransom her and see what we can get. It's up to you, Thomas."

Eleanor looked to the night sky. This was not going the way she had hoped. She still had one more card to play. She didn't want to, but needs must.

"You may have heard of me by a different name. My parents call me Eleanor, but some people call me Nel. You may have heard of that name before?"

Thomas looked slightly less cocky. "Nel? I don't think so." And then his face paled. He said, "Black Nel?"

"Yes, some people have called me that. I had hoped to let it go, but it seems that I am not permitted to forget my past."

Thomas was shaking. The fat man and his wife were looking confused, but not so Charles. He said, "Black Nel, Thomas, Black Nel! The bounty on her is enormous. Forget these trinkets. Let's tie her up and take her in. We could be rich!"

"I really wish you hadn't said that."

The knife left her hand before Thomas could react. Within a second it was embedded in Charles' throat. He fell from his horse, his lifeblood pulsing away through the wound in his neck.

Thomas looked ashen but went for his pistol. Eleanor was too fast and used his own sword to slash the palm holding the pistol and then pointed the tip, dripping blood, at his throat.

"I'm sorry." He said, frantically looking to where Charles lay motionless on the ground. "We didn't know who you were. We would have never…"

"Never what? Never attacked us if you knew who I was? Black Nel or Lady Eleanor, it should make no difference. Yet, here we are."

"I'm sorry, m'Lady, truly sorry. We are new to these parts."

Eleanor shook her head in disgust at the stain appearing on the front of his breeches.

"I have spent years leaving behind the persona of Nel. Years re-building my life, moving away from the darkness. And now you have exposed me. I cannot let that pass."

"Please ma'am, I wouldn't have allowed Charles to turn you in. Honestly." The stain was nearly at his knees and his breeches hung from him. There was a smell of effluent that hung in the air.

"I almost believe you. You are so young. Why did you enter this game?"

Hope shone in his eyes. "I grew up poor, this was my only way to live a decent life."

Eleanor shook her head. "I did it for adventure, for notoriety, for fame. But in all the years that I rode the highways, I never killed an innocent person. I never humiliated anyone the way you did this poor man and his wife."

Thomas took off his coat and offered it to the lady to cover herself. "I am so sorry," he said to her, "I don't know what came over me. Please, forgive me."

"They may forgive you in time," said Eleanor, "But I cannot allow to pass unanswered such an attack on guests of my house. I believe you when you say that you are sorry but, had I not been here, who knows where your lust and greed may have led you? Your most heinous sin, however, is the use of 'Stand and deliver' and 'Your money or your life.' Such phrases only appear in picture books and do little to glamourise your actions."

The sword flashed, and the frilled collar on his shirt turned red. He grasped at his throat and sank to his knees, his eyes round, looking at her in terror.

"I'm sorry, too," she said, "but only because you chose this night to ply your craft."

Thomas fell backwards, dead, and Eleanor sighed.

"Perkins?"

"Yes, m'lady, a terrible business for sure."

Faithful Perkins, her loyal companion, with her during her adventures, and now installed with his family on her estate where he was employed as her driver and protector.

"Tie their horses to the back of the carriage. We will leave their bodies here to be found as footpads."

"Yes, m'lady. As you suggest."

Perkins went about his work and then used a large branch to remove the horse prints.

The obese man was beside himself with gratitude. "My lady, I cannot tell you how thankful we are. You have saved us from the scum that tried to do us harm." To emphasise his words, he kicked at the body on the floor and spat with disgust.

His wife, however, remained silent. Wrapped tight in the coat that Thomas had provided, she looked at Eleanor, her whole body shaking.

"I'm so very sorry." said Eleanor. "I had hoped for a pleasant weekend for all of us, and this has ruined it for everyone."

"It is no problem to us, my dear", said the man. "You were simply wonderful. What a tale to be told."

His wife looked at him and shook her head. "We know who she is, James. She cannot let that pass."

"Perkins, you need to take the pistol and shoot me. In the arm, I think, the fleshy part."

"Yes, m'lady. I would suggest the left arm if that is acceptable to you?"

"I suppose it matters little where you choose but, yes, if you insist."

"That's good, m'lady, because after I have shot you, you will need to stab me in the shoulder."

"Do you really think that is necessary, Perkins?"

"Yes, m'lady. For Mrs Perkins would have me roasted over hot coals if she thought you were injured, and I had not nearly died trying to save you."

"Ah, yes, we had better not let Mrs Perkins loose on you."

After it was done, the carriage continued on its journey to Crowle house where Eleanor's family had lived for generations. Behind them, four bodies rested in evidence of a tragic misadventure as a man died trying to save his wife from highwaymen but retained honour in killing the bandits before succumbing to his wounds.

Chapter 17 - The Lift

The lift came to a shuddering stop with a screech of metal which was almost painful. The four people contained within looked around in various degrees of alarm.

"What was that?" Macy looked terrified.

"I think we've just stopped. No doubt we'll be going again soon." The elegant man in the suit smiled at her. "Don't worry."

Macy wasn't convinced and looking at the man, she was pretty sure that he didn't know anything more than she did. She moved to the buttons and pressed "G" repeatedly.

The lady in the pink coat put her hand on Macy's arm. "I don't think that's going to help. The lights on the panel are out, so the power must be off."

"The main lights are still on so there must be power somewhere." Macy looked around in terror. This was her worst nightmare. As well the rest of her issues, claustrophobia was a real trigger. Why hadn't she taken the stairs like she normally did? The lift was beginning to look like a prison.

"What's your name, love? I'm called Sherry. Like the drink."

Macy looked at her and was calmed by the way Sherry smiled at her. "I'm Macy."

"Ok, Macy. You don't need to worry. I've been trapped in lifts like this before. They'll have us out in no time. You'll see."

The man in the suit nodded his agreement. "These things are as safe as houses these days. It's the escalators you need to worry about, not the lifts. My wife told me a story about a woman who was on an escalator in Marks & Spencer wearing Crocs. Her shoes fell off and she got her leg trapped in the mechanism. It was nasty. I've always used lifts or stairs since. I'm Tony, by the way."

If he wanted to make Macy feel better, he had sadly not read the room. "Oh, bloody thanks for that, Tony. That makes me feel *so much* better. Not."

The fourth member of the group was a young man of about twenty-five, wearing a green parka. He scratched the straggly hair on his chin. "My name's Luke. When I was at college in Doncaster, they had signs in the stairwell that said: 'To avoid the risk of heart attack, use the stairs going downwards, and the lifts going upwards.' So that's what I always did. "

"That seems weird." said Sherry. "Surely students are fit enough to walk up and down stairs without having a heart attack?"

"It was a Technical College that catered to people of all ages. There were some real oldies there, and some of the teachers were ancient."

"Something will have happened." said Tony.

Sherry looked at him. "What do you mean, something happened?"

"Someone will have had a heart attack walking up the stairs. They put up notices like that when they're trying to cover their backsides. My wife is a Health & Safety inspector, and she told me that most of the notices you see are because something has happened, and they must be seen to do something about it. Risk assessments are the thing these days. You've got to cover all the bases."

Macy looked at them in horror. Was she in a different place, or had she stepped through a reality portal or something? "You're all wittering on about risk assessments and Crocs and heart attacks, but we are still stuck in this bloody lift. We need to get out of here!"

"Aw, don't you worry, love. Things like this happen all the time. Before you know it, we'll be out of here and laughing about it." Sherry put her arm on Macy again and seemed surprised when Macy just shrugged away from her.

"You can all say what you want, but if the power is off on the panel, it means the lift is broken. We don't know whether we're stuck between floors and, if we are, it's going to take longer for them to get to us. It could be a broken switch, or there might be a real issue with the cable. What happens if it breaks?"

"I've heard about this." said Tony. "If the cable breaks, it's best for us all to jump up and down together. That means there's a fifty-fifty chance that we will be in the air when the lift crashes to the bottom. Maybe we should do that anyway?"

"Yeah, that's bollocks." said Luke. "It's a common misconception and it's likely to get you killed."

"I'm sorry," said Tony, "I got this from a very reliable source."

Luke grinned. "Someone in Health and Safety?" He smiled when Tony blushed. "The thing is, if you're jumping, you are still travelling at the same speed as the lift that's falling. By jumping, you're trying to hang in the air so that you only have a small distance to fall, but in fact, you're more likely to smash your head on the roof of the lift than save yourself."

Tony was not deterred. "Well, if we fall, I'm still jumping."

Sherry looked at the two men with disgust. "Can you both shut up about ropes breaking and lifts falling? Can't you see that Macy is scared out of her wits. It doesn't do anything for her, or me, with you two trying to see who has the biggest dick. Just stop it, ok?"

It was true. Macy was scared. She could feel the walls of the lift closing in on her. She wondered how much air was left in this lift and whether it would be enough for them all. She already felt light-headed, and she knew she had to get out of this coffin as fast as she could. She looked around frantically until her eyes fixed on something on the roof. A vent. A way out.

"Can one of you blokes give me a leg up so I can see if we can get that vent open? If we can get out, there's always a ladder in these shafts, and we could climb out. It would be better than being cooped up in this place with the air running out."

Sherry shook her head. "Oh, I don't think that's a good idea, Macy. I think we should just wait here until they come for us. They won't be long, love, you'll see."

"I think she's right," said Tony, "there's no point taking risks when we don't have to."

"Says the man with a Health & Safety wife." laughed Luke. "Come on, Macy, I think it's a cracking idea. It'll be like John McLane in Die Hard. We can pretend we're in the Nakatomi Tower instead of this crummy shop. I'll give you a leg up." He linked his hands together and Macy stepped into them.

As he lifted her up, her leg was shaking, and she realised this wasn't going to be as easy as she first thought. The vent was fixed with two large bolts with a flat head. She thought fast. "Has anyone got a two-pound coin?"

Tony put his hand in his pocket and pulled out a selection of coins. "Here, I've got one, but I still don't think you should be doing this." He reluctantly passed the coin up to Macy who immediately started using it to loosen the bolts. It was hard, but eventually, the first one came out. The second bolt was much tighter, however, and she struggled with it.

Luke was also struggling. "Macy, I need to let you down for a minute. My arms are killing me."

Reluctantly she accepted being lowered to the floor. "I hope you recover soon because I need to get out of here. I can't stand being trapped in here much longer."

Luke laughed. "We're obviously not very good company. Maybe if you took your shoes off it would help. They were digging into my hands last time."

"No problem, I just want to get out. Are you ready?"

He nodded. She kicked her shoes off and climbed back onto his waiting hands. This time she was more determined and, after applying as much pressure as she was able, the bolt became free. "Look out below!"

The vent cover clattered to the floor and they could see up into the lift shaft. "There's a ladder!" Macy cried. "I'm going to climb out and get to the ladder. Lift me just a bit higher."

Just then, the lift shuddered. The main cable vibrated and sang, and the lights came back on the panel. "Macy, come back inside." said Sherry. "The lift is working again, we can get out normally. Come on, it's all ok now."

Macy looked reluctant but, when Luke lowered his hands, she had no choice but to jump down. Sherry pressed the glowing green "G" button, and the lift shuddered once more before beginning its descent to the ground floor.

The lift stopped gently, and the doors slid slowly open. Outside stood four men dressed in black from head to foot. Black boots, black overalls, and black balaclavas with only their eyes showing. Dark eyes, covered in sunglasses. It wasn't the black that was most intimidating, however, it was the guns. The front two carried Heckler & Koch MP5 submachine guns, and the rear two were equipped with Heckler & Koch G36 rifles. All the guns were pointing towards the inside of the lift. Both Tony and Luke started to back away in fear before one of the black-clad policemen rasped, "Don't move. Stay exactly where you are."

The two men in the lift complied immediately, all bravado gone. Sherry turned to Macy and said, "Macy Adams, I am arresting you on the suspicion of multiple counts of theft and fraud. You do not have to say anything. But it may harm your defence if you do not mention when questioned something which you later rely on in court. Anything you do say may be given in evidence. Hands behind your back."

Macy turned her head and spat on the floor in front of Sherry before doing as she was told. As the handcuffs clicked shut, she said, "I should have known you were a pig. There was a filthy smell in this lift. How did you know?"

"We picked you up on store CCTV. You're getting careless, Macy, not like you at all. Scoping out your next mark, were you?"

As they led Macy out of the lift, Detective Sergeant Sherry Dawson leaned across to the leader of the armed officers and whispered, "You got here just in time. We nearly lost her. She was headed out of the roof when the lights came back on."

Chapter 18 - The Toilet Seat Wars

"Bloody hell, I'm sick of this!"

Anna walked into the bathroom and could feel her cheeks burning. *He did this on purpose. Bastard.*

The toilet seat and lid were up because he had used it last. Her eyes burned and she felt a hot tear squeeze out and run down her cheek. She hated him. Everything about him.

The toilet seat was a symptom, not a cause, she knew that. It started out with her leaving the lid up after she had been to the toilet. He didn't like that. Said that it caused an aerosol when she flushed, and he didn't want to breathe in her waste. So, when she wanted to annoy him, she would deliberately leave it up. Men are so easy. After a while, though, he started leaving the lid and seat up in retaliation. She had been to the toilet at night more than once and sat directly on cold, wet porcelain. Hearing him laugh when she screamed was even worse than having to get cleaned up.

She was glad he wasn't home so he couldn't see her getting annoyed. That would be too much. She wished she'd listened to her mum when she said she shouldn't marry him. Her family could see what he was like but, she was young and in love, and she thought she knew better. That was thirty years ago. Her mum died ten years ago and had never changed her mind about him. Anna missed her mum.

It had been fine at the beginning. More than fine. They were great together and had a fabulous life. It started to change after the difficult birth of their second child. Something must have been damaged because Anna went off sex completely. It wasn't just that she was exhausted from looking after too young kids on her own because, of course, he couldn't be expected to help as he had such a busy and tiring job. Even when she was on her knees crying, unable to see beyond the next few minutes, desperate for rest, he didn't help. She didn't know how she would have coped if her mum hadn't been around to help.

His affair started that year, the first of many. They should have got divorced then, but they worked through it together for the sake of their young family. She went to the doctor, but nothing helped. Now, the kids were gone, young families of their own. But Anna and her husband were still together, taunting each other, living together because it was easier than the alternative.

The hot tears started again as she put the lid down after she finished. It was easier to prevent the arguments and, despite him thinking she left the lid up to wind him up, it was because she genuinely just forgot most of the time. She washed and dried her hands, annoyed that, again, she was doing what he wanted. Still, it was better than fighting all the time. She was halfway down the stairs when she turned around and went back into the bathroom where she quickly turned the toilet roll around so that it dispensed from the back. Smiling to herself, she went about her day.

"What's for dinner?" He kicked off his shoes and put on the slippers waiting for him.

When Anna was young, her dad often said the same thing to her mum who, in an accented Irish brogue would typically reply, "Shit on a shovel!" This was a game that they both played and enjoyed, and there was never any animosity between them. Anna couldn't tell whether her husband was asking the question in malice, or simply because it was what he always said when he got home. She preferred to think it was the latter and answered, "Shepherd's Pie and Broccoli. Afterwards, I have got some of those Portuguese Tarts you like. We could have some squirty cream with them if you fancy it?"

The dinner went well. He was unusually talkative, telling her all about the new chap at work who they had been teasing. The usual stuff – sent to the stores for 'a long weight', to the workshop manager to ask for 'a sky hook'. It was the same nonsense that had been going on for years, but Anna felt herself laughing along, torn between feeling sorry for the young lad, yet wanting to enjoy the moment.

She decided to try her luck. "There's a new season of that police thing with Anna Maxwell Martin in starting tonight. Shall we watch it?"

"I can't. Going out this evening. Don't know when I will be back."

And there it was. Again. There was no point asking him where he was going. "Ok, no problem." She stood up and gathered the plates to stack in the dishwasher. The tears would come later. She wasn't going to let him see.

"You need to leave him."

Her sister meant well, but she couldn't understand how difficult it was. "It's not that easy, Erin. What about the girls, what would they think? Where would I go?"

"Ella and Lou are both old enough to not be bothered. They've seen the same things the rest of us have, and they don't want you to spend your whole life miserable."

"But he's their dad. I can't do that to them."

"Anna, they can love their dad, and they can love you too. Even if you aren't together. It's not like they are teenagers anymore. You could come and stay with John and me until you get yourself sorted."

Anna loved the weekly meetups with Erin in Costa. She loved the almond croissants, chocolate twists, and vanilla latté she ordered every week, even though she knew she would have to work off the extra calories later. It was something she could look forward to, something to cling to.

"I can't get divorced. I know you think I should, but I can't."

Erin put down the cup she had just lifted to her lips. "Why not? You're living a lie at the moment. "What on earth makes you want to stay with him?"

Anna looked around to see if anyone was near before whispering, "I'm scared."

"You're scared of him? Has he hurt you?"

"No, no, nothing like that. When we argue, it's his words that hurt. He has never raised a hand to me."

"Then what are you scared of? You could start a new life, you're young enough, maybe meet someone new."

Anna looked around again. "It's my fault. I can't."

Erin's eyes were wide. "How on earth is it your fault? Are his affairs your fault?"

"No, well, maybe. After Lou was born, I wasn't really interested in, you know, S. E. X. anymore."

Erin shook her head. "Aw, sweetie, that isn't your fault. Is that what this is all about? You have a low libido?"

Anna flushed. "You can't blame him for having affairs if he isn't satisfied at home. With me."

"Anna, he was having affairs before either of your girls were born. When you were pregnant. Before you were married. Why do you think Mum tried to persuade you not to marry him?"

Anna flushed. "I know what people say, but I trust him. Trusted him anyway. I don't think he would have done that before my problems started."

For the first time, Erin looked angry. "When your problems started, did he try and help you? Go to the doctor with you to try and find a solution?"

Anna was angry too. "It wasn't like that. I was embarrassed. I didn't want to have to explain to a doctor about my issues."

"That's what doctors are for! You could have gone to a female doctor!"

"It's not that easy. After Lou, and what happened, I didn't want any more children. Because of the difficulties, the doctors told me I couldn't use hormonal contraceptives. I love my kids, but, look, this is difficult…"

"Anna, you do know it takes two to tango, right? He could have used condoms. He could have had a vasectomy if he was that bothered."

"He didn't like to. Said it didn't feel right. I wish he did have a vasectomy. It would have solved more than one problem."

"What do you mean?"

Anna looked at her sister and, this time, couldn't stop the hot tears running down her cheeks. "He has a son."

"What the fuck are you talking about?"

"He has a boy with another woman. I only found out when I saw regular payments going out of our account to someone I didn't know. I challenged him and he admitted it. He was quite proud of it, actually. The boy's name is Jared. I've never met him, but the girls have. He's apparently very nice."

Her sister looked at Anna and shook her head. "How long have you known?"

"About ten years. When we switched to online banking."

"He's a bastard. Through and through."

Anna dressed nicely for dinner. She told her husband at breakfast they needed to talk and, to her surprise, he agreed. All day she had been nervous. She couldn't settle. Housework, prepare dinner, go for a walk, read for a while, take the dog for a walk. All of it was done on automatic as she prepared for the evening.

"Do you want a divorce?" She forced the words out through the frog in her throat. Instead of answering straight away, he finished the trifle he was eating. He didn't even look up. *Infuriating man.* When he had finished eating, he made a show of wiping his mouth, and then took a long gulp from the Chablis she had chosen for the occasion.

"Divorce? It's a bit too late for that, isn't it? Maybe twenty years ago, but I can't see any point in it now."

Anna set her chin. She was determined not to be bullied. "I'm unhappy. I never see you. When we are together, all we do is argue."

"You're unhappy? What about me? Twenty-five years I've put up with you not being a proper wife. If anyone should be looking for a divorce it should be me."

Pushing her buttons, straight away. "I know what you are talking about, and I'm sorry, but we can't change the past. Neither of us chose this, and that's why I think we should end it. We would both be happier."

"Where would you go?"

"I wouldn't go anywhere. You would. Go and live with your son's mother for all I care."

"You're not having this house. This is *my* house. I paid the mortgage with my wages. You'll have to go and live with your bloody sister and her useless husband."

Anna had been waiting for this. Her solicitor had told her what would probably happen. "It will be split fifty-fifty by the courts. Everything will. All savings, the house, your pension."

He spluttered, "My pension? You can fuck right off. I've worked for that, not you. You're not having any of it. I'll go to court, and I'll tell them everything about you, how you've not had sex with me for twenty years."

Anna sighed. "I wouldn't expect anything less. Of course, We'll also have to tell the judge about your affairs. Tell me, honestly for once, were you seeing other people before the kids were born?"

His laugh was full of bravado. "I fucked your maid of honour the night before we got married. Your best friend. She said I was the best she ever had. All of them did."

The dagger hit home, but Anna was astonished that she was able to maintain control. "Ok, thanks for confirming what I was told. I'll speak to my solicitor and get things put in motion."

The bluster was gone. "You've got a fucking solicitor? You're serious about this?"

"Yes, I am. You should get a solicitor too."

"Fuck you, bitch, I'm going out!"

The next four months were horrendous. Living together, but further apart than ever before. When he was informed by his solicitor that the information Anna had been given was correct, he became even more sullen. Even the prospect of a day in court to humiliate Anna became less attractive when he was told it would only cost more money. It was far better to sort out the financial arrangements before it went to court.

When he learned that Anna intended to buy him out of his half of the house with her share of his pension, he stopped talking to her entirely. Little annoyances started to increase as time went on. Cupboards left open, toilet seat never lowered, empty toilet rolls never replaced, lights left on. Anna moved through it all. She continued to wash and iron his clothes, always making enough for him to eat, even if he wasn't in most of the time.

Erin was delighted, and somewhat astounded at the change in her sister. "I never thought you would go through with it, Anna. I'm so proud of you."

Anna slowly stirred her coffee and looked at her sister. "It was you who finally made me see sense, Erin. You gave me the push I needed."

Erin put her hand on Anna's. "It will be all right, you know? He's just a bully, and he never thought you'd have the nerve to leave him."

"Yeah, I know. I'm so glad that I took the first step. I just can't wait for it to be over."

"What will you do when you are divorced? What will he do?"

"Well, I don't really care what he does. I've spent so long worrying about how I can do things right for him, it will be a relief to not need to care. He will be ok. As for me, I have booked a cruise to Norway to see the Northern Lights. My life starts here!"

"That's my girl!"

The crash from upstairs was loud and sudden. Anna thought at first there had been an accident outside, but quickly ran upstairs when she realised it was inside. "Are you all right in there?"

When there was no response, Anna pushed open the bathroom door. Something was blocking it, but she managed to squeeze inside. What she saw made her retch and then scream. He was lying on the floor with the toilet seat underneath him. There was blood running down the cistern and, when she put her hand to the back of his head, she felt the sticky wetness of an open wound. *Oh my God, Oh my God. Talk to me, open your eyes!*

When the paramedics arrived, they found her still there, holding his lifeless body, her blouse wet with a combination of blood and tears. They had to pry her hands away, but they didn't attempt resuscitation, there wasn't any point.

"The evidence points to the deceased becoming a victim of his own attempted practical joke. It is the opinion of this court that the screws holding the toilet seat in place were removed by the victim with the intention of catching his wife unawares. There does not appear to be any evidence that the deceased intended harm to his wife, but rather this was a silly prank aimed at humiliation in a series of petty and unfortunate events occurring over the months preceding the accident. It would seem that he forgot his own trap which resulted in this tragic and needless death. The verdict of this court is accidental death."

Erin squeezed Anna's arm and whispered, "You must be glad that's over?" Anna nodded through her tears. "Yes," she whispered, "I didn't want this to happen, any of it. I just wanted to be happy." They stood up to leave, and Anna put her hand in her coat pocket. Inside, she squeezed the four screws sewn into the lining of her coat. Four screws to change a life. Four screws for freedom.

Chapter 19 - The Incident at A&E

Well, being at A&E at 11:00 pm wasn't on my Christmas bingo card, but here I am. The knee finally gave way, even the walking stick didn't help. Tried to climb a couple of stairs and instead ended up in a heap on the floor. It bloody hurts too.

I'm now in a cubicle waiting for a doctor to see me, but I've been told it won't happen for ages. At least it's moving forward. When we first arrived, the paramedic told me we were in a queue behind fourteen other ambulances, and we would probably be here all night. And this is after a five-hour wait for the ambulance to arrive. As new ambulances arrived, they occupied the waiting spaces behind us. It was weird seeing them. As they parked, they must have turned the engine off because they all had a brief flash of the blue's and two's.

There must have been some sort of triage going on because there were paramedics moving all over the place and trollies being taken out of vehicles behind ours. I suppose that people who had heart attacks or strokes would have to be dealt with first. I should have felt sorry for them, but my leg really hurt. The paramedics gave me some gas and air, but they wouldn't give me any other pain relief in case a doctor decided I needed to have an operation.

Eventually, they put me in a wheelchair and wheeled me through to the main A&E reception. I was a bit pissed off that we weren't going in through the ambulance doors, but what do I know? As it happens, the receptionists got me through pretty quickly. Not before I saw the mess in the rest of A&E.

God, it was a microcosm of nationalities and ethnicities in there. It was packed to heaving, and I must admit I was glad that I didn't have to spend too long in there. There was food and used wipes all over the place, and nobody seemed to be bothered about clearing it up. People were coughing, and there were people who were obviously either high on drugs or pissed up. Maybe both. In the short time I was in there, a fight started but the security got on top of it pretty quickly. Security in A&E! You wouldn't credit that society has got so bad we need security in these places.

I couldn't get over how packed it was. The paramedic told me a lot of people come to A&E these days with minor complaints because they can't get a doctor's appointment. Looking at some of the people here, I can well believe it.

And then there's the vapes! People can't smoke at the hospitals anymore, so they go and stand in the doorway and get high on vapes instead. And the smell - pineapple, cherries and all sorts of other bloody stuff blowing back into the room when the door is opened. I can smell it on me too, my clothes got covered in it on the way in. It's worse than smoking. It should all be banned. Hospitals should be for sick people, not just scroungers and people who can't get an appointment with their own doctor. I remember when the NHS was a beacon to the rest of the world. Now it's full of knackered staff who run around trying their best to help people.

And the smell of these people. Oh God, the smell. Sweat, vomit, shit – all mixed in a foul miasma that the bleach just can't cover. And the moaning. Bloody hell, my leg hurts, but you need to learn to keep your mouth shut – grin and bear it like my old dad used to say. Some of these people are worse than footballers, the way they cry and moan. It gets in your head and drives you mad. When did people start to get so weak?

There was a bloke walking around talking to himself. Bit scary, to be honest. He was marching up and down in straight lines whispering to himself. People like that shouldn't be in A&E. "Accident and Emergency" – the name says it all. If you haven't had an accident, or your condition isn't an emergency, bugger off and leave the place for those of us who really need it.

Anyway, like I said, I didn't have to suffer the indignity of being in there too long before they moved me to a cubicle. I've been in here for about four hours now, and still no doctor. My cubicle is straight opposite the main ambulance entrance (that I wasn't allowed in) and it's been like Piccadilly Circus. People are being brought in constantly and there are doctors and nurses running around. The ambulance crew that brought me in came back with someone else about an hour ago. I nodded to the paramedic, but I don't think he saw me.

There was a load of action about two hours ago. A woman came in carrying a baby. She was screaming and crying, and the baby looked blue, to be honest. She had all her family with her, and they all ran after this little Asian doctor who led them down the corridor. It was quiet for about three or four minutes, and then a baby cried. Everyone clapped and cheered. I would have joined in, but my leg was really giving me loads of pain. Still, proves what the NHS can do, even when underfunded.

There's an old woman in the next cubicle, she's driving me crazy. It looks like she fell over and banged her head, so they're doing all sorts of tests on her. The thing is, she must have dementia or something because she can't remember anything and keeps repeating the same things over and over again.

"Where are my keys? Have you got my keys? I need my keys to get into my house."

The woman with her is her daughter, I think, and she must have the patience of a bloody saint. She keeps telling the old girl that there's nothing to worry about and she's got the keys. No matter how many times she gets asked, she never gets mad. I don't know how she does it. I think the daughter was trying to get some sleep in the chair a while ago, but the mother woke her up and told her to get upstairs to her proper bed. The old girl thinks she's at home – I don't think she has any idea that she's in hospital or what's happening. There are coppers and prison warders walking by her cubicle, and she keeps asking the daughter what the police are doing in her house. I don't ever want to end up like that.

Some progress. A doctor popped her head in, took one look at my leg, and decided I needed a scan to see what's going on with my knee. She looked really stressed and didn't stay longer than about thirty seconds. They wheeled me away to get the scan, and now I'm back in my cubicle. The old dear is still in the room next door, and she's still asking about her keys.

I can see the doctors and nurses through the curtains. If I didn't know any better, it would be easy to believe there was only one doctor working. Impossible in a hospital this size, but it makes you wonder. I hope she gets the results of my scan soon and comes in to tell me what's going to happen.

Three hours I've been waiting, and still no doctor. The old lady has gone now with an all-clear. She banged her head, but there is, apparently, no lasting damage. The paramedics told me we would be here all night, but I thought they were exaggerating. One good thing, though – they finally gave me some painkillers. Paracetamol and Codeine are all I'm allowed, but it has taken the edge off. A pretty nurse brought it in with a cup of water but didn't seem very interested in chatting. I must have lost my touch.

"Mr Jackson?"

Finally, a doctor. It's a good job I wasn't in for something really serious because I would have been in trouble, I think.

The doctor is the Asian woman who dealt with the baby. She looks harrassed.

"I have looked at your scans, and your knee is going to need surgical intervention. We are looking for a bed on a surgical ward and you will be transferred as soon as arrangements have been made."

"Well, you're not telling me anything I didn't know. When will the operation be happening?"

"That will be up to the surgeon to decide. It won't be today as it is now Christmas Day, but it needs doing soon."

"What about afterwards? After the operation, I mean?"

"You will need three to four months of intensive physiotherapy before you are able to walk again."

I'm laughing now. I can't stop the grin spreading across my face.

"Most patients aren't pleased when told they need major surgery."

"You jammy bugger, Tommy."

The doctor is confused and looks to the warder to explain.

"Tommy is close to release on license after fourteen years inside. Staying in here over Christmas and then three months of physio will take him nicely to his release day. Almost as if he planned it that way."

Chapter 20 - The Christmas Miracle

"Bollocks to Christmas and all who sail in her!"

Palmer pushed someone dressed as Santa out of the way and tried to fight his way through the crowds. He burped and laughed at himself. Christmas was about getting pissed, buying loads of stuff, half of which doesn't get eaten, buying presents in the vain hope that it will make someone happy, and generally doing everything to excess. *And all these people had decided to do it today when he was just trying to get home.*

He staggered against a lamppost, the effects of too many lunchtime drinks starting to show when exposed to the cold air. He grinned again. *Bah humbug!*

The street was absolutely packed with people doing last-minute shopping. Despite the Christmas music blaring from the shops, desperate to entice buyers in before the sales started, despite the bright colours and flashing lights, Palmer thought there wasn't much of the spirit of Christmas about. People looked stressed, harassed and generally unhappy. The only people who looked immune to the chaos were the drunks like him, in plentiful supply on the afternoon of Christmas Eve.

He thought about waiting for a bus but decided it might be better to get a taxi. Unfortunately, the taxi rank was at the other end of town. He wasn't processing thoughts as quickly as normal, so weighing up the alternatives took him a while. A bus would be cheaper but would take forever. Could he get home without needing the toilet? A taxi would be more expensive, and he would have to walk through all these people to get to the taxi rank, but it would be so much nicer. *Sod it! It's Christmas!*

When he was a kid, all the Christmas decorations were paper chains which his mum hung from the corners of the room to the chandelier in the middle. His dad used to complain about the drawing pins stuck in the walls but then, he complained about most things. He hated Christmas too, so it's small wonder that it lost its wonder for Palmer. There were lights on their Christmas tree, but they were pretty basic. The sort that wouldn't work if one bulb was faulty, or not screwed in properly.

The decorations today are much better, of course. Technology made everything multicoloured and cheap, and it seems anything is possible. You can easily find the lights to match your theme - gold, silver, blue, or anything else. The main Christmas colours of red and green were still all over, of course, as mandated by the Coca-Cola company and their version of Santa Claus.

You can now buy a tree with all the lights embedded-ded to suit your fancy. Cheap enough that you could throw it out and get a new one each year. Palmer remembered an old friend who used to move his fully decorated tree into a spare room every January and cover it with a sheet. Every December, he would then move the tree back into the living room for the duration of the Christmas period. He was into recycling before it became a thing. Of course, he could only get away with this after his wife died – she wouldn't have put up with any of that nonsense. And now he was gone too.

Too many of his friends were gone. Palmer caught sight of his reflection in a window. Overweight, saggy jowls, grey hair. He was hardly a picture of health. And old. Old and alone. He shook his head to relieve the doldrums and pressed on, determined to reach the taxi rank before the pubs threw out at 3 pm. It would be impossible to get a cab after that.

The church in the town centre stood apart from the shops. As he walked towards it, he could hear singing and could just see a choir practising through the open doors. Christmas Carols. For a moment, he considered going in but decided against it. It was a long time since he had been to church, and now wasn't the time to start going again. He walked past the closed street next to the church and changed his mind. *Maybe it would be a good time?* He turned back and walked right up to the church door. The choir were dressed in robes and looked like angels from the top of a Christmas tree.

"Silent night, Holy night, all is calm, all is bright…"

Palmer smiled. It was always the best one. Years ago, when he was much younger, he was part of a choir that sang in The Arndale Centre every Christmas to raise money for various local charities. Christmas Eve was always the best day, especially after 3 pm. The drunks would come out of the pubs in generous moods, fuelled by the drink. Almost without exception, they would request the choir to sing 'Silent Night' – the song of Christmas that made everyone think of their childhood. Tears would flow, and the donations would rise. Not coins any longer, but notes – five, ten and twenty-pound notes. The choir would make as much in the hour after the pubs closed as they would throughout the rest of the day. And, by the end of it, they would be sick of 'Silent Night.'

This version, however, was beautiful. Such a simple song, but the layered harmonies were uplifting, and he caught himself remembering a simpler time. *Bloody song. Who's the drunk now?*

Palmer pulled himself together and set off walking towards the taxi rank. As he passed the alley next to the church again, he heard a cat howling. He had never been a fan of cats, his family had always kept dogs, but he still hated the thought of any animal in distress, so he stopped and turned into the alley to see if he could help. There it was again, coming from the boxes piled up against the church wall. He wasn't sure if it was a cat now. The sound was different close-up. He pulled down the lid of the box where the noise came from and almost choked. It wasn't a cat. It was a human child, wrapped in a blanket. *What the fuck?* Palmer had no experience with kids and was totally out of his depth. Instinct took over, however, and he lifted the child out and held it awkwardly against his chest before walking back out of the alley.

Nothing had changed. The street was still crowded. Palmer looked around franticly, searching for someone who could help. People didn't even look at him as they passed, and he started to panic. He pulled out his phone and dialled the emergency number.

"Hello, which service do you require?"

"Err, police, I think."

After confirming his details, he was transferred to the police operator.

"What is the nature of your emergency?"

"I've found a baby, in a box."

"Please confirm, sir, you have found a baby?"

"Yes, in the alley next to St Wilfred's church on the high street."

There was a pause. "Can you please confirm if the child is alive, sir?"

"Oh, yes, sorry, I should have said that. The child is fine."

"Please stay where you are, sir. Responders will be with you shortly."

Palmer felt self-conscious waiting, but he had certainly sobered quickly. He saw lights in the distance, and then a police patrol car pulled up next to him after only ten minutes, followed a short time later by an ambulance.

"Mr Palmer? Could you please pass the baby to my colleague and then join me in the car?" The police officer wasn't smiling and looked rather stern. The WPC with him, however, had a kinder face and smiled as she took the baby from him before handing it gently to the waiting ambulance crew.

The policeman opened the rear door of the car and invited Palmer to step inside. He put his hand on Palmer's head to assist him, and then walked around and got in the other side of the car, next to him. He removed a notebook and pen from his top pocket and addressed Palmer directly.

"In your own words, sir, could you please describe the circumstances regarding your discovery of the child?"

Palmer did as he was asked, telling the officer exactly what happened.

"At what point did you hear the child crying?"

"Well, at first, I thought it was a cat, not a child. I mean, who leaves a kid out on their own, especially on Christmas Eve? I was just walking past, and I heard the noise, so I thought I had better check."

"Sir, we have a witness who says that she saw you walk past the alley on three occasions. Can you confirm this?"

"Three times?" Palmer was confused at first and then it dawned on him. "Oh yes! I was walking towards the taxi rank when I heard singing in the church, so I turned back and went to listen for a while. It was when I came back that I heard the baby."

"So, you could hear singing in the church but not a baby crying?"

"Well, no, I suppose it wasn't crying the first time I went past."

"Can you tell me where you had been prior to this incident?"

"I was in the pub. Kings Arms on the High Street. Last day of work before Christmas, it's tradition."

"And how much did you have to drink?"

"I dunno. Quite a bit, we'd been there a while."

"Can you give us the names of people who might corroborate what you are saying?"

Palmer shrugged, confused. As he passed on the names of his colleagues and the policeman wrote them down in his notebook, he wondered for the first time what was happening.

The policeman said, "Were any of these colleagues involved in this incident?" He paused. "Did they, perhaps, dare you to do something as a prank?"

Palmer was stunned. *He thinks I am behind this!*

"No! I told you. I was just walking past and heard the crying. You can't honestly think that I've got anything to do with this?"

Judging by the face of the constable, that's exactly what he did think.

Palmer was saved from further cross-examination as the door opened when the WPC returned. She addressed her colleague, "John, we've found the mother. She was here all the time watching. She came across when she saw us arrive."

She led Palmer out and took him to the ambulance. The baby was in the arms of a young girl, probably no more than seventeen or eighteen. Palmer shivered. "It's shock, let's get you checked out."

Thirty minutes later, he was wrapped in a blue blanket and sitting on the footwell of the ambulance with the WPC. The ambulance crew had checked him out. They had given him the all-clear, along with an admonishment to not drink so much in future.

"It's Phil Palmer, isn't it? Used to go to St Hilda's school?"

"Err, yeah. Do I know you?" Palmer looked at the WPC but didn't recognise her.

"Ellen Cross. I was a bit different then. You might remember my pink spiky hair?"

"Bloody hell, that was you?"

"Yes. A rebel to the core. And then I joined the police force!"

"Well, we all dreamed of changing the world, didn't we? And then we became adults."

"I have a confession to make. It was me who gave you your nickname."

"Peepee? Ha, don't worry, people have been calling me that for years."

"Well, that makes me feel better."

"I seem to remember trying to give you a Christmas kiss outside the Woolpack. You were in uniform, I was pissed, and I don't think your colleague was too impressed either."

She laughed. "I do remember. And you did get a kiss! It was the highlight of my Christmas."

"Yeah, right."

She laughed. "It was! Listen, is there anyone you need me to call? Family?"

"No, it's just me. Mum died five years back and, since then, it's just me and the dog."

"I know what you mean. I was married a long time ago, but I got hurt at work, which stopped me from having children. My husband at the time couldn't cope. He never wanted me to be a police officer, and after I got hurt, he wanted me to leave the force, but I wouldn't."

"Wow, St Hilda's has a lot to answer for! Listen, I know you probably can't tell me, but what about the baby, what happened?"

"Well, it's a bit sad, really. The baby is fine, very healthy and well looked after."

"So why was it left in an alley?"

"The mother is very young. She was watching all the time to make sure it was all right, but she wanted this to happen. She wanted to get the police involved."

Palmer was confused. This didn't make any sense.

"I don't understand. Why would she do this?"

Ellen looked around before continuing. "The girl is sixteen. But only just sixteen."

"So, she was fifteen when…"

"Yes, that's what we assume."

"But I still don't understand why she would do this. Especially on Christmas Eve."

"That's the thing. If she's telling the truth, the child's father is a priest at the church. No one believed her, so she wanted us to get involved."

Palmer felt the bile rising in his stomach and started retching. He couldn't help himself. He tasted acid in his throat before his stomach convulsed and expelled its contents in a pile on the floor. He wiped his mouth with the back of his hand, embarrassed.

"I'm really sorry."

Ellen looked at the floor and the splashes of vomit on her boots before pouring a bottle of water over it to swill it into the nearby grate.

"It's ok. Probably a result of shock and a heavy combination of alcohol."

"No, it's not that. Well, maybe the bit about the alcohol is true. What you said brought back memories."

"Of school?"

"No, well, about that time. When you said what happened to the girl."

He looked at her and couldn't stop the tears.

She put a tentative hand on his arm. "It's ok, it's horrible. It will get sorted."

"No, you don't understand. It happened to me too. Not a priest, a youth worker. But it happened a long time ago. This brought it all back. I don't blame that poor girl for what she did. It's wrong. I hope it doesn't fuck her up the way it fucked me up."

"Oh, Phil, I'm so sorry. I didn't realise."

"How could you? It's why I never got married, never had kids. I couldn't see any way that I'd let a kid of my own be exposed to that."

"Fuck. I am so sorry. Did you ever tell anyone? Was the person ever exposed?"

"No, it's like I said, it was a long time ago. Who would have believed me anyway? I was just a kid."

"I'm sure the authorities would have done something about it, Phil."

"Really? Even today nothing's changed. That's why that poor girl had to pull a stunt like she did tonight. It's not just the church. People in authority always have the upper hand."

Ellen put a hand on his shivering palm. "You're not wrong. But we do what we can."

"Sorry, Ellen, I didn't mean to say that you were responsible."

"I know. It's ok. Listen, what are you doing tomorrow, Christmas Day?"

Palmer was taken aback by the sudden change in subject. He looked at her, and she smiled back at him.

"Pizza, probably. King's speech, Disney film, and fall asleep in the chair."

"Sounds lovely." She hesitated. "Why not come and do that at our house? There's only me, mum, and dad. But you'd be very welcome."

Palmer looked at her, trying to remember the girl with pink hair, but seeing instead a smiling, friendly woman, probably with as many cares as him. He looked for pity in her eyes but saw only warmth.

"Can I bring Shona?"

"Err, yes. Who's Shona?"

"My dog, of course, she gets lonely if I am out too long."

Ellen laughed. "Yes, of course, but I hope she likes cats."

"She's not like me. She likes everyone and everything!"

"Sorted then. And in the new year how about we both see if we can help each other to sort out the demons in our lives?"

Palmer smiled. Maybe it would be a happy new year after all.

Acknowledgements

I would like to thank everyone who has helped to get this book to this stage. From the Open University, my tutors Rosemary Dun and Lucy Yates, and the course lead Dr Ed Hogan who all contributed to helping me to write a little better.

To the people who helped enormously by proof-reading at all stages of the development, especially Gill & Dave, Alice and Danielle.

To all my family, both close and extended – Mum, Steve, Michelle, Sean, Stuart, Alice (again!) and James – thanks for putting up with me.

To friends that I have made in the creative world. Fhi (I can now work on the other thing!), Alison and so many talented others. I look forward to following your careers.

To Matt Gemmell for producing the Ulysses export styles which make formatting so much easier, and for being patient when I needed a little extra help.

Finally, of course, to my ever-suffering wife, Eleanor, who has supported me throughout this endeavour, and gave me the push to pursue writing as a serious habit. Thank you.

Printed in Dunstable, United Kingdom

66097635R00130